Journey to the Pole

For thrills and adventure
readers everywhere love

Peter Lerangis

ANTARCTICA

Journey to the Pole
Escape from Disaster

WATCHERS

#1 LAST STOP
#2 REWIND
#3 I.D.
#4 WAR
#5 ISLAND
#6 LAB 6

ANTARCTICA

Journey to the Pole

Peter Lerangis

SCHOLASTIC INC.
New York Toronto London Auckland Sydney
Mexico City New Delhi Hong Kong

ISBN 0-439-16387-0

12 11 10 9 8 7 6 5 4 3 2 0 1 2 3 4 5/0

Printed in the U.S.A. 40
First Scholastic printing, June 2000

For David Levithan

Acknowledgments

I began researching this book while waiting long hours to be selected as a juror, so my first thanks go to the New York City criminal court system. Anne Fadiman, my good friend and an avid Antarctic buff, provided great enthusiasm and much research material from her amazing personal library. The real Peter Mansfield, whom I've had the good fortune of knowing for twenty-five years, helped enormously with nautical terminology. I thank the real Larry Walden for his patient tutelage during several summer afternoons sailing on Casco Bay. And my mother, Mary Lerangis, who sent me to Greek school when I was a kid and shouldn't have had to correct all my Greek language mistakes, nevertheless did so with joy. *Efharistò, s'aghapò.*

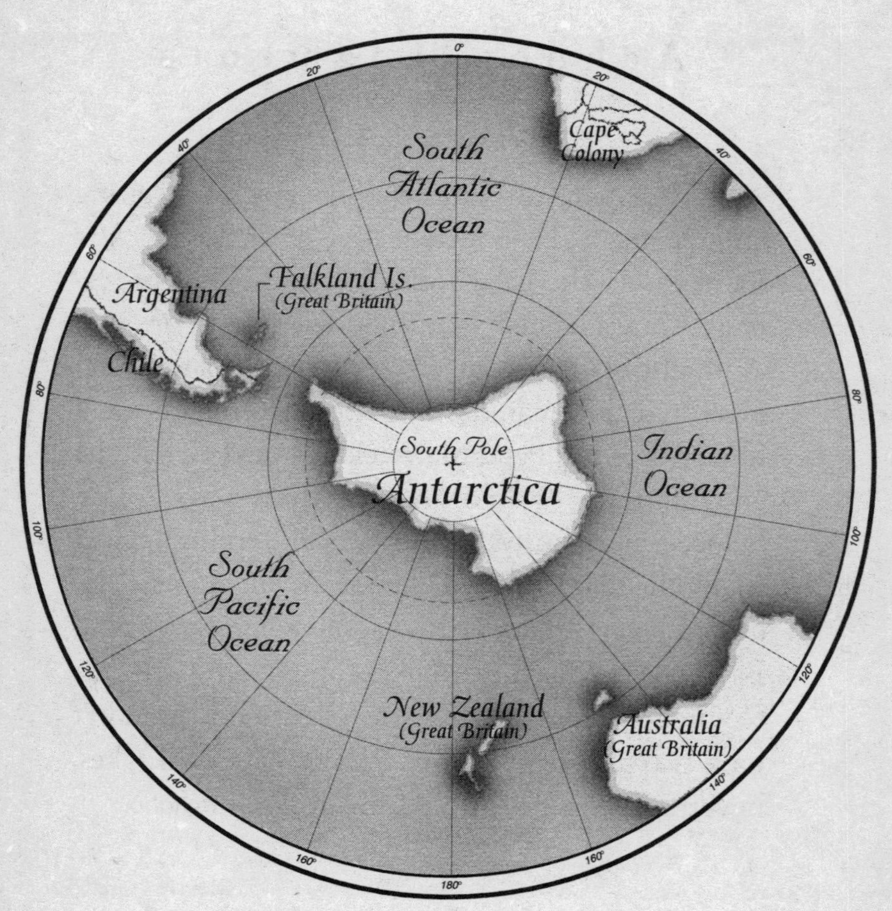

Antarctica as it was in 1909.

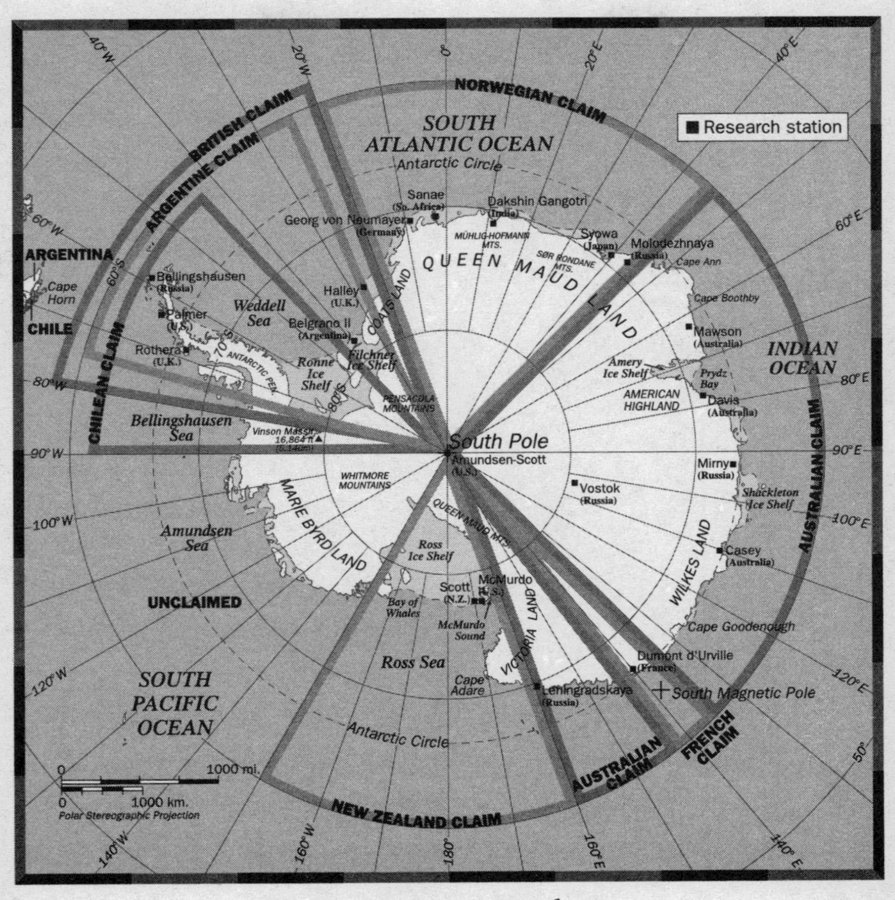

Antarctica as it is today.

Prologue

"I can be so bold to say no man will venture further south than I have done, and that the lands to the south will never be explored." — *Captain James Cook, English explorer, 1774.*

The call of Antarctica is loud and clear:

Go *away*.

You hear it in the groans of colliding ice floes. In the shriek of 200-mile-an-hour winds hurtling down the Transantarctic Mountains. In the thunder of an ice shelf splitting into the sea. In the hostile silence of a darkness that begins in April and ends in June.

You feel it, too, as the temperature drops to –100° F. and your breath forms a mask of solid ice inside your hood. Standing still can kill you, and you fight off the urge to sleep, because you know you may never waken.

You see it in the landscape, a slab of ice so

heavy — twenty-four quadrillion tons — that it flattens the contour of the earth. So vast that you can walk the distance from New York to Seattle and never touch ground.

To sail there, you must cross the world's most savage sea, the only body of water that circles the planet unobstructed by land. On the way you may see an image of the bleak terrain, a lifeless mirage reflected against the ice crystals of a frozen sky.

Antarctica is a fortress. A desert. A prison.

Captain Cook called it as he saw it. But his prediction was wrong.

After him, many more came. In the 1800s, they came in ships, discovering coastlines, landing on shores. By the early 1900s, the British explorers Robert Scott and Ernest Shackleton penetrated into the interior and began dreaming of the impossible: a voyage to the South Pole.

By 1909 Shackleton had come close. Scott was planning another attempt. So was a Norwegian, Roald Amundsen.

No American had attempted to reach Antarctica in almost eight decades. No one had the skill or the interest to join the race to the South Pole.

Or so it is thought.

In a city that was daily stretching its borders

from river to river, the father of two boys was setting his sights south.

Like many, he had heard the call: *Go away*.

And he had found it irresistible.

The boys were Colin and Andrew Winslow, of 37 Bond Street, New York, New York. Their father's name was Jack.

This is their story.

Part One

Before

1

Colin

Colin Winslow ran through the canyon streets of lower Manhattan. He ran even though his chest hurt and the rain pelted him and his feet slipped on the wet pavement. He ran because on May 8, 1909, at a little past 5:20 in the afternoon, his world had ended for the second time.

His stepmother was dead. It happened while he and Andrew were watching, while they held her hands in the hospital room. She woke from a sleep, called Father's name, and closed her eyes. Just like that, the pneumonia took her, and Colin felt his heart squeeze, exactly the way it had when his mother had died. Suddenly the hospital walls couldn't hold enough air for him, so he ran.

He had to find Father.

Father was downtown with the Fat Man. Colin didn't know where the office was, so he ran home to find out. People on the street yelled at him, and the old ones tsk-tsked, but he didn't care.

You weren't supposed to run in New York. You were supposed to walk, tip your hat to the ladies, cross at corners. Cities had rules, and Colin had always liked that, the way they gave order to chaos. You could feel safe and small, folded in among the grim, purposeful faces; the buildings framing low, soot-gray skies; the faint, familiar stink of fish and horse dung and tannery hides. In his old home in Alaska, the sea and the snow and the cruel, killing waters had reminded him of his mother. Here in New York he'd thought he could bury the pain.

Now he knew he'd been wrong. Wrong about it all. He'd been living in a dream, and only now, at the age of sixteen, did he finally realize the truth: The bad things always found you, and the streets of New York were stone and brick, as gray and flat and ugly as Harwinton, Alaska. In New York you died the way you lived, not by an accident on the sea like the one that had taken his mother, but by something passed quietly in a crowd, a tiny germ that ate away at you until your lungs flooded and then collapsed.

Colin stepped off the curb to cross. He heard a screech to his right, and an automobile skidded, just avoiding him.

"Hey, you overgrown coolie! Aren't your eyes big enough to see where you're going?" From a leather seat the driver glared down at Colin. The man's back was ramrod straight, his whiskers drooping in the rain.

Colin kept going, and so the man said what men like him usually said: *Yellow-skin, slant-eye Eskimo, go back where you belong.* You got used to it here, if you didn't look like the People Who Owned Things, the light-skinned ones like Father. Colin resembled the People Who Did Things — caught the fish, sailed the seas, built the houses. He was six feet tall like a Winslow but small-necked and broad-shouldered like his mother's family, like an Inuit, with massive hands and a lumbering, rocking gait.

He didn't turn back, he didn't feel like answering or throttling the guy. He felt nothing.

Just past the blacksmith Colin turned left onto Bond Street. Number 37 was in the middle of the block, and he leaped up the stoop to open the front door.

"Father!"

The darkness swallowed his call. He raced past

the parlor entry and yanked open the door to his father's study.

It smelled of cherry pipe tobacco and hair tonic. Father's worn leather chair was angled back from the desk. The drawers had been pulled open and papers were piled helter-skelter. A fan blew in from the open window, causing the stuffed Arctic tern to swing lazily from the ceiling on its string. The moose head stared from the fireplace.

Colin ran to the desk to look for a clue, a note, anything that might hint where Father was.

Samuel Breen, Shipwright, Bill for Labor Pursuant to Construction of Barquentine *Mystery* . . . United States Government Topographical Map and Report on Antarctic Continent . . . *Frank Leslie's Illustrated Weekly*, "The Mad Race to Conquer the South Pole" . . . April 21, 1909, List of Able Seamen and Officers, Port of New York . . .

The papers blurred. Colin blinked away tears and swept his arm across the desk. The contents flew onto the polar bearskin rug. He wanted to burn it all, the rug, the maps, the bills, the stuffed animals. All the reminders of polar travel past and future. Of Antarctica, the obsession that had consumed Father's energy and kept him from home, kept him from the deathbed of his own wife.

As Colin's eyes focused, he saw a note on top of all the others:

HORACE J. PUTNEY ENTERPRISES, LTD.
176 FRANKLIN STREET
NEW YORK, NEW YORK

BY MESSENGER

Jack,
I think we can make a deal. I am in today until 9:00. Putney

Franklin Street. That was in the Red Light District.

Colin had never been there. You never went there after dark if you valued your life. What did the Fat Man do for a living anyway?

Colin ran out of the house and barreled down Broadway. It was a long run, at least a mile, and as he crossed Canal Street the sun set behind the tenements and the smell of decay rushed up from the pavement. Fire escapes creaked as if craning to watch him. Figures slithered and turned in the doorway shadows, and a cry exploded from above, strangled and anguished, growing to a shrill laugh. A shapeless blob hurtled to the street from a third-story window and exploded on the cobblestones, a mass of rotted food and rank liquid that oozed into the gutter, from which two animal eyes peered upward, green and greedy.

Corner to corner, Colin told himself. Eyes front.

As he turned onto Franklin, the storefronts advertised goods in languages he didn't recognize, and broken carts stood chained to hitching posts. The distant din of angry voices grew closer.

Colin strained to see numbers above the doors — 119 . . . 121. . . .

At the end of the wall of shadows, a crowd had gathered in front of a tavern. A man lay across the pavement, his face bloodied, while a group of burly men pulled off an angry attacker. Two mounted constables rode up, brandishing billy clubs, followed by an ambulance.

Just beyond them, where Franklin Street met Varick and West Broadway, a small, pristine brick building stood on the corner. Its light shone through stained-glass windows protected by steel bars. It was clean and jewellike, completely out of place in this wretched neighborhood.

It had to be Putney's office.

Colin took a wide berth around the drunken brawl and crossed the street.

2

Jack

Putney was the money man.

It was that simple.

To go to Antarctica you needed a ship. One with a hull thick enough to withstand the pressure of the ice. A prow even thicker to batter icebergs without cracking. A steam engine and at least three masts, one or two of them full-rigged. Also a science lab, living quarters for up to thirty men, a kitchen, a cargo hold for a year's worth of provisions, and enough kennel space and food for three dozen or so large dogs.

Jack Winslow would provide the leadership, the vision. But someone had to pay.

His old Harvard friends wouldn't. They were rich enough now, but they hadn't taken Ol' Good Time Jack seriously. They never had.

After months of failure and mounting debts, Jack had turned to Putney as a last resort. Putney was a crook by all accounts. He'd made his fortune in the tenements, crowding people who didn't speak English into buildings that couldn't hold them. His expensive lawyers had protected him in the courts, but even Putney couldn't buy the thing he wanted most: a good reputation.

Jack offered it. Putney would share the glory. The newspapers would make him a national hero, the financier of the greatest American voyage ever made — the greatest voyage ever made, period.

The deal had been quick and easy. Strictly business.

Jack dreaded having to break it.

"Cigar?" Horace Putney pushed a gilded box across his desk. Above him, a lazy ceiling fan made eddies of the dust and smoke, which were tinted by the stained-glass windows that blocked sight of the squalid streets from inside his countinghouse. "Havana. The best."

"I'll pass," Jack said with an impatient smile.

"To the point, then — Iphigenia has pneumonia. She's taken a turn for the worse."

Putney leaned forward, his chair groaning with the weight. His starched white shirt settled against the desk, like an iceberg against the hull of a ship. "If there's anything I can do . . ."

"I'm afraid, Horace, that I must call off the trip."

There. Cards on the table.

"Well." Putney's brows creased upward. "Jack, I understand how upset you must be. Whatever care she requires, I'll make sure she has it — the best doctors, help for the house — you can prepare the voyage while you're with her."

"Horace, this may take a while."

"Fine. A week, a month, two months, whatever it takes. Hire a good captain and delegate responsibility to him —"

"There is no time. Shackleton came so close — and Scott can taste success. He's gathering a crew already. I wouldn't doubt that Amundsen is doing the same. If the trip is to be done, it must be done now, heart and soul. And I simply can't. What if she doesn't pull through, Horace? I flee to the South Pole, leaving my sons alone? What kind of man would do that?"

"Have they no relatives to stay with while you're gone — your in-laws in Boston, perhaps?"

"We haven't spoken to them for years. They cut off contact —"

"I'll find them for you. I have ways."

"That isn't the point —"

"Then what is? You've been a man possessed, Jack. The ultimate frontier, the greatest moment of glory in American history — what happened to all that? Not important anymore?"

"The point is family, Horace. The point is loving someone more than yourself."

The man wouldn't understand, of course. He was unmarried, childless, obsessed with wealth. He had never loved anyone more than Horace Putney.

Putney raised a skeptical eyebrow. "I must say, I hadn't prepared for this."

"I'm sorry, Horace. I understand it is a bitter disappointment to you —"

"Not to me, Jack. I'll survive. But you? There are practical matters to think of. Samuel Breen, for one."

Jack had been expecting this.

His life had been about Breen these days — stalling him, telling him the money was on its way. Breen was the finest shipbuilder in the Northeast.

Though Jack had no cash, Breen had put up a fortune of his own money to buy a sturdy barquentine from a Norwegian company — and another fortune to refit it to Jack's specifications. It would be called the *Mystery*, and it would "sail through granite." But Jack hadn't repaid a penny yet, and Breen was already threatening to sue.

"Cover Breen's costs, Horace," Jack said. "You won't lose money. He can sell the ship and split the proceeds with me. I will pay you back every cent."

"We had an agreement, Jack. No trip, no money." Putney gave a heavy shrug. "I can recommend a good bankruptcy lawyer . . . if you can afford him."

"And if I can't?" Jack said, rising to his feet.

"Your choice," Putney replied. "I hear conditions in the poorhouse are conducive neither to good health nor to the proper upbringing of young men."

Jack lunged across the desk. But a pair of strong arms grabbed him from behind — Putney's butler, ever prepared for emergencies.

Obviously Putney was no stranger to personal attacks.

"You are a viper," Jack said through clenched teeth.

Putney rose and met Jack's glance. "Perhaps,

Jack, you are not seeing all the possibilities. You could, for instance, take the boys with you."

"They're sixteen and fifteen," Jack said. "They're in school. They have no experience."

"They're healthy, smart, capable young men," Putney replied. "And besides, they'll have Philip to look after them."

"Philip?"

"My sister's boy. Twenty-one or so. An able sailor, I hear tell. They live in England, and she's sending him here — supposedly to benefit from my example. I believe he'd profit more on your ship, as would you."

"The selection of crew is *my* prerogative —"

"And make sure none of the men know the real destination until you reach your first port of call in South America. I want no leaks, no word getting out to Scott so he can try to hurry his voyage to beat you."

"That's ludicrous. The men need to know where they're going —"

"One other thing — I reserve all film and photographic rights. After all this, I think I deserve to make a bit of a profit, don't you think?"

A sudden smack on the front door made all three men turn.

The door flew open, letting in a blast of cold air and a familiar broad silhouette.

"Colin?" Jack said.

"Father," Colin blurted out. "I have bad news. . . ."

3

Andrew

May 22, 1909

"Name?" Andrew asked.

"Berle," the man answered.

Andrew began writing. "That's *B–E–R–L — ?*"

"Not *Berle*," the man shot back. "*B–O–Y–L–E* — Berle!"

A few of the other men snickered.

"Any experience working on a three-masted ship?" Andrew pressed on.

Boyle nodded. "Soitenly."

The front room exploded with guffaws and catcalls.

Andrew didn't mind. They could talk with their strange accents, sing sea chanteys, drag their muddy boots across the Persian rugs, reek of unbathed flesh. Only nineteen would be kept out of the hundreds who had answered Jack's posting for positions on the *Mystery*.

Number 20 would be a photographer, to be chosen tomorrow. Numbers 21 and 22 were Andrew and Colin. They were going to the South Pole.

Andrew still had to pinch himself, just to be sure he hadn't dreamed this up. Every day he'd expected his stepfather, Jack, to come to his senses. To break the news that the trip was canceled, or that Colin and Andrew would be staying in Boston with Grandmother and Grandfather.

But this morning, on Andrew's sixteenth birthday, Jack had told the boys' teachers they'd be gone for a year and arranged for the appropriate books to be loaded onto the ship. Everything was full steam ahead.

Andrew knew why this was happening. Surely it was Mother's plan. She had wanted the trip to happen. She must have spoken to Jack before she died, insisted that he shake off his grief, hold fast to his dream — and take along his sons.

By now Andrew had read seven nautical manuals, a boat-building book, and every word Jack

London had ever written. He would be as good a sailor as any of the men in this room.

They were the last interviewees today. Jack's posting had been nothing spectacular. "Good wages, New York to Buenos Aires." No word about Antarctica. That part was to be secret. And yet in three days Jack would have seen 467 of them. They'd come from as far as San Francisco. Many would be spending the night in Central Park.

If the truth had been out, the men would be lined up to the Hudson River.

Antarctica was on everyone's tongue these days. The men were talking about Shackleton now. Shack had just returned from his second attempt on the South Pole. He'd come within 112 miles, the closest anyone ever had. Some were saying he was all show, no grit. Others claimed he had come within 100 yards and lost courage.

Fools. Shack was good, one of the best. Andrew knew about them all, each man and milestone — first sighting (Cook, Briton, 1774); first Antarctic islands discovered (Bellinghausen, Russian, 1819–21); first landing (Davis, American, 1821); first ship trapped in ice (de Gerlache, Belgian, 1897); first failed attempt on the South Pole (Scott and Shackleton, 1907).

He was aching to explode the men's mistakes, to tell the men the truth about the voyage and watch the looks on their faces. But he had an agreement with Jack. The destination was secret.

"Gentlemen, please keep the noise down — an interview is going on in the parlor." Andrew pointed to the next man, the only one he hadn't yet signed in. "Name?"

"Orailoglu," the man muttered.

This time Andrew estimated the spelling. "Thank you. Kennedy will be next!"

Kennedy sat up straight and smoothed his suit jacket. He had a gaunt face with thick red hair and hands that looked too big for his body. He seemed a decent sort, a Southern boy, and he had excellent credentials as ship's carpenter. "So who are you, sonny, the captain's son?" he asked.

"My stepfather is the expedition leader," Andrew explained. "He will choose a captain. I am junior officer."

"Ah," Kennedy said.

"Didn't know they had nurseries on these ships," Boyle muttered.

Andrew quietly wrote a dark *NO* next to Boyle's name.

* * *

The last of them left at 6:50. Jack stood against the jamb of the parlor entrance, his eyes red and droopy. "Happy birthday. Sorry you had to work so hard."

"One hundred forty-three men today," Andrew announced. "Kennedy, I thought, showed promise —"

"Was there any theft?"

"I don't think so. I brought everything inside that wasn't bolted down."

"Good. Well. Let's forget about them for a moment, shall we? I have a surprise for you. We're going to celebrate. Where's your brother?"

Andrew glanced over his shoulder toward the kitchen. "I asked him to bring in some tea for the men."

"When?"

"Three hours ago."

"Come along." Jack walked into the kitchen. Colin was sitting at the table, poring over the latest *Frank Leslie's Illustrated Weekly*. "Colin, what are you doing?"

"Reading," Colin said.

"What about that tea?" Andrew asked.

"Those guys weren't tea types."

"So you just stayed here and didn't bother to help out," Andrew said.

"Why should I?"

"Because you're part of this, Colin. Because a crew is only as good as its weakest member —"

"And which of us would *that* be?"

"I'm talking about cooperation. Teamwork!"

"This trip wasn't *my* idea —"

"At ease, men!" Jack put his arms around both sons. "If you stop yammering a moment, you may see Raschke trying desperately to enter the house."

Chef Raschke, who lived in Number 35, was leaning on the front door, holding an enormous roast goose from his restaurant. He had a pink, doughy face and a belly that hinted at the joys of his profession.

Jack pulled open the door. "Karl, that's entirely too big for us."

"Ah, I forgot you're only three now, ain't you?" Raschke said, bringing the bird into the kitchen. "Well, eat up anyways, in memory of the missus. And happy birthday, young master."

Raschke set the goose down and ran off to work.

The thick, smoky smell of sage and thyme slowly permeated every room. As Jack carved, Andrew set the table, leaving a place for Mother.

He wasn't ready yet to erase her from dinner. In a few weeks maybe. It was still May.

The night was unusually cool, and Colin built a small fire in the hearth. As they sat to dinner, the room was festive and warm with the smell of smoking birchwood.

As Jack began the grace, Andrew tried to avert his eyes from the empty seat at the foot of the table.

On special occasions, Mother had always sung the grace.

None of them could carry a tune — Andrew, Colin, Jack — so they would listen. Her voice was a gift, like cool, rippling water. They'd ask her to repeat the grace again and again. It was a tune she had invented and set to a Wordsworth poem:

> O, *dearest, dearest boys! my heart*
> *For better lore would seldom yearn,*
> *Could I but teach the hundredth part*
> *Of what from thee I learn.*

"We give thanks for this meal," Jack began, "and for another year in the life of my stepson, and we pray for his and his brother's health as they approach a voyage that will try their courage and strength. . . ."

Colin rolled his eyes. Andrew kicked him under the table.

"Most especially, we give thanks for the life of our beloved Iphigenia, who is with us here in spirit —"

Jack's voice caught.

Andrew held his breath. He could feel her presence. The air to his right seemed displaced somehow, as if she'd dropped in unannounced.

He heard an *Amen*, saw a plate being lifted from the table. *Happy birthday, pass the peas, please.*

Why? Why had it happened? She had been alive, happy and laughing, then three days later she was gone. What had she done? What could *he* have done to make things better? For what were they giving thanks today?

He felt the room swirl. The goose seemed to be sliding down the table.

Buck up, Andrew told himself. *Steady now. Be positive.*

Raising his glass, he bolted up from his seat. "I propose a toast — to — Mother's memory."

"Hear, hear!" Jack and Colin chimed in.

Andrew downed his water, then with a smile excused himself to the washroom.

For a long while he stood, looking at his ashen face in the mirror, catching his breath, counting his breaths, wiping his mind clean.

Completely clean. The past is out of your control. What you can't control can control you if you let it. Better to bury it and move on.

He slapped himself once, twice, until he saw some color in his cheeks. Then he opened the door and walked back toward the dining room.

"Everything all right?" Jack asked.

"Fine," Andrew said with a smile.

From outside a loud whinny interrupted his response.

"And good riddance to ya!" a hoarse voice shouted.

A hansom cab had lurched to a stop at the curb. The door opened and a young man stepped out. He wore a full-length fur coat, a black bowler, and patent-leather shoes, and as he stood on the sidewalk, he rapped a carved ivory walking stick on the side of the cab.

"My bags?" he demanded.

"No tip, no bags," the driver replied.

"A gratuity is given as a token of appreciation for service above and beyond — not for surly behavior by louts who can't find their way around the neighborhood and yet easily manage to locate every pothole therein."

The driver hopped off his seat and disappeared behind the cab. "Ya want your bags?" his voice called out. "Here's your bags!"

One by one, four leather suitcases came hurtling over the top of the cab, landing with wet thuds on the sidewalk. One of them opened, spilling out piles of freshly laundered white underwear.

"And keep yer money!" the driver said, tossing down a handful of coins as he leaped back in the seat and spurred on the horses.

"You will hear from my barrister!" the young man shouted, waving his cane. "This is an outrage!"

Jack stood up and moved toward the door. "That," he said, "will be Philip."

Part Two

Departure

4

Philip

May 30, 1909

"Her eyes are like two stars so bright,
Her face is fair, her step is light,
I'll go no more a-rovin' from you, fair maid:
A-rovin', a-rovin', 'cause rovin's been my ru-eye-in,
I'll go no more a-rovin' from you, fair maid. . . ."

The singing. Anything but the singing.

The personal odor of these men was almost as dreadful as their breath, which reeked of codfish not quite digested. They'd knock you over before walking around you, and their language alone was enough to guarantee their eternal damnation.

But the singing, as far as Philip was concerned, was the worst.

Half of them were tone-deaf. The other half didn't know the words but joined in nevertheless with peculiar rhythmic grunts. And all sang with such gusto and joy, one would think the *Mystery* were about to sail to some glorious Caribbean island.

In a few months they'd all be fingerless with frostbite, wiping penguin droppings off their boots. How many of them would be singing if they knew that? No more a-rovin', indeed.

On the dock, girlfriends and relatives waved tearfully, shouting their undying love. Uncle Horace, of course, was not among them. Philip did not miss him.

The ship itself was a ghastly mess, its floor — *deck* — piled high with coal for the engine.

"Hey, you boy!" called a sailor who was hanging off one of the masts. "You by the taffrail! Go to the fo'c'sle, will you, and tell 'em we're needing to replace the mainsail sheet!"

"It's Westfall," Philip shouted back. "*Mister* Westfall to you. And I am on security duty."

"In the stern? What are you guarding against, an attack by the Statue of Liberty?"

Cheeky. They were all so cheeky.

Philip made a show of looking at his clipboard and quickly walked toward the gangplank.

Fo'c'sle. Philip knew that word. It was short for forecastle, where the sailors lived — just under the deck at the front of the boat. No. Front was *bow.* And it wasn't a boat, it was a ship — *she* was a ship. You were supposed to call it *she.* The other words — taffrail? mainsail sheet? — were Greek to Philip.

Read up on sailing, Uncle Horace had said. *I told them you knew what you were doing.*

He hadn't wanted his nephew around. Fine. Then all he needed to do was set Philip up in a bachelor apartment in some genteel neighborhood. They'd never have to cross paths. But this — a voyage to the bottom of the earth — was insanity.

Mum had warned that Horace was strong-willed. But he was more than that; he was treacherous. Threatening to report Philip to the British authorities was below the belt.

That wouldn't do. Especially since Philip was hiding from them.

So he shut up. And he stayed with the Winslows. And he pretended.

They were odd, those Winslows. The overgrown one, the one who looked vaguely Asian, hardly said a word but ate enough for three. There was something wound-up about him, and Philip knew to steer clear. The glory boy, Andrew the Poet — he'd been running around all morning, battening down hatches or whatever a sailor did. For all his high spirits, you'd think he was going off to war. Detestable.

Did they suspect the truth? Philip wondered. They must. Surely Mr. Winslow suspected. His eyes showed that. And he made certain to give Philip all the easy jobs. Easy and boring.

Today he was to "check attendance" of all the sailors and officers reporting for duty.

As Philip approached the gangplank, a man lumbered up, loaded down with baggage, much more than the allowed amount. "This is not an ocean liner, sir," Philip said. "Only two bags allowed. Sorry, but I didn't make the rules. Do you have the proper papers?"

The man had piercing black eyes that became slitted and wary. "The name's David Ruskey," he said. "Mr. Winslow will vouch for the luggage —"

"Your papers, please."

The man dropped two duffel bags and unhooked two more from his shoulders. Leaning over, he opened a bag and pulled out a sheaf of papers.

The bag was full of camera equipment.

Uncle Horace had told Philip to watch the photographer, to make sure no one stole any of the negatives or film. People would pay good money for the photos and films of this expedition, and Uncle Horace owned all the rights.

"Delighted to meet you, sir," Philip said genially, taking a five-pound note out of his pocket to hand Ruskey with the papers. "I know you'll be taking so many photographs that you wouldn't miss one or two from time to time. . . ."

Ruskey glanced at the money, gave him a baffled look, and stuffed it into his pocket. With a gruff nod, he picked up his equipment and moved on. Philip checked off his name.

The man seemed woefully honest, but you never knew. No reason not to see some personal profit from this torture.

"Hey, P.W., it's about time!" Andrew's voice cried out. "Where have you been? The men tell me they're climbing aboard without anyone to greet them."

P.W. What an awful sound. Like a reaction to a bad smell.

"And you actually believe them?" Philip said with a haughty laugh. "They're toying with your mind . . . A.D.W. They'll do that to the hopelessly naive. Watch out."

"But — but —"

Philip turned away. That one was so easy to fluster.

Now another man was climbing the gangplank. Very self-important. Tweed jacket, pipe. He was over six feet tall, trim and broad-shouldered, a salt-and-pepper beard outlining a square jaw. A bit long in the tooth — forty-five or fifty, maybe. Pathetic to be that age and still working the poop decks.

"Papers," Philip demanded.

"Barth," the man said, angling to go around Philip. "Elias Barth."

Philip stood in his way. "Very impressed, I'm sure. But unless you can show me your papers, I must ask you to get off my ship and return to the nearest pub whence you have no doubt come."

The man trained a pair of icy-blue eyes on Philip.

"Of course," Philip said, "if you're willing to part with a five-spot, I could see my way to taking you presently to Mr. Winslow —"

Elias Barth dropped his bag, grabbed Philip's shirt, lifted him off the deck, and held him like a sack of flour as he walked to amidships.

"Unhand me!" Philip shouted. "Mr. Winslow!

Help! He's going to throw me overboard. I CAN'T SWIM!"

"The sea is too good for you, deck rat."

Philip felt a cold steel pole against his back, a metal hook poking into his neck.

Barth released him. The hook caught his shirt, causing it to pull up painfully under his arms — and Philip hung over the deck, his legs flailing.

The men were gathering about, laughing. Andrew and Colin, too. Ruskey had taken out a small camera and was snapping a photo.

"Get me down!" Philip yelled. "He can't do this! Report him! His name is Elias Barth — do you hear me, ELIAS BARTH!"

The men were guffawing now. Doubling over.

"What is so blasted *funny*?" Philip demanded.

"Elias Barth," said Andrew, "is our captain."

5

Jack

September 5, 1909

"Gentlemen, please, be quiet," Jack announced.

Off the starboard hull, he could see the port of Buenos Aires slowly come into sight. The sun was strong, raising a sweat on his brow.

The men were rambunctious today. Packing their bags, singing, bragging about the women they intended to meet in port, barely paying him mind.

Jack didn't blame them. The trip to South America had been a disaster. Half the men had been flattened by gastrointestinal sickness near Panama, and Captain Barth had worked the rest to the bone. Having three boys aboard hadn't helped matters.

Andrew had been trying hard but was only getting in people's way, Colin had remained sullen and reluctant, and Philip was deadweight. Putney had lied badly about the boy's age and experience; he was a landlubber, sixteen or seventeen years old at most, and the men hated him. Everyone had been exhausted and short-tempered — and now they believed the trip was over. Of course they were excited.

Captain Barth stepped onto the makeshift lectern, a tackle box, beside Jack. "*Button it, boys!*"

"What's the news, Pop?" cried Sam Bailey, a wiry, fast-talking sailor.

"You bought us bon voyage gifts?" shouted Bruce Cranston, whose dark good looks made him seem more matinee idol than seaman.

Jack smiled wanly. He needed these men. The port would be full of sailors looking for work, but few would be experienced enough to withstand the desolation of Antarctica.

His mind reeled when he thought of how much had to be done in port — dogs loaded, kennels built, food bought. Five crew members had promised to meet them here — a doctor, a veterinarian, a geologist, a biologist, and a dog handler. With them, the total crew would be thirty, including the captain and himself. It was a crucial amount. Enough to do all the work, enough to split into teams.

Jack cleared his throat. "Men, we are moments away from our first port of call on a long voyage. We will dock here for a week and then continue on to our ultimate destination."

He told them everything, and they listened. As the words flew out of his mouth, Jack felt his voice rising and falling like a preacher's, and he reminded his men that they were all headed for the earth's last undiscovered frontier, that their names would go down in history books. That within a few months, Old Glory would be flying on the South Pole.

When he finished, the men were silent.

"A joke, right, Pop?" Pete Hayes finally piped up.

"He's straight," Bailey muttered.

"Good of you to tell us!" shouted Vincent Lombardo, a man broad of beam and loud of voice.

Bailey shot back, "You wanted an engraved invitation, Your Highness?"

"Wait. What did he say?" Brillman, the electrician.

"You mean, we can't leave?" Sanders, a sailor.

"Says who?"

"Shut up and listen to the man!"

It was chaos. They were shouting one another down.

"Quiet, or I will dock your wages for a week!" Captain Barth shouted.

"We will be gone perhaps a year," Jack said. "We will travel during the Antarctic summer, when the sun is in the sky nearly all day and temperatures may reach as high as thirty degrees Fahrenheit. But it will be dangerous. The sea can freeze around the ship. Even after we land, we will cross much terrain that has never been charted, in weather that can change in an instant. I've planned with great care to provide enough stores to last through the bitterest conditions. Sailors, I will pay your commissions even after we have anchored. When that happens, we will split into teams — half the men will stay on board, the other half will journey with dog sledges to the Pole. I will determine the teams when we arrive, based on what I observe during the voyage.

"The choice, gentlemen, is yours. I selected only the best for this trip — men with character, temperament, strength, and the freedom of spirit to succeed. My commitment, above all others, is to do everything in my power to bring my men home alive. I will brook no man too wary to take extraordinary risks — but I will allow no risks foolhardy enough to jeopardize a life. That is my vow.

"Should you choose to disembark, go with our blessing. I am, after all, asking you to commit to something no man has done before. Should you stay, you will earn more than my gratitude. The country will rise up to thank you for the rest of your lives.

"All I ask is that you consider."

In the quiet that followed, a bell buoy clanged. Seagulls cawed greedily overhead, scoping for food, and distant music sounded from the shore.

The men's faces were blank.

"Cat got your tongues?" Captain Barth said. "Come on, give us a show of hands — who will stay aboard ship?"

No one raised a hand.

Jack's heart stopped. He would have to replace them all. It would take months. It was an impossible task.

Colin had been right. The trip was doomed.

"Pop?" Kennedy. The carpenter.

"Yes, sir?" Jack said.

"Begging your pardon," Kennedy said, "but will we have to eat penguin? And if so, have you considered laying in a couple cases of ketchup?"

The first mate, Siegal, was the first to laugh.

Lombardo followed, a big, brassy honk. His hand shot in the air. "Count me in, Pop — straight to the bottom of the world!"

"To the bottom!" Hayes called out. He was an enormous man, and as he thrust his fist upward, it seemed to rise to the yardarm.

"To the bottom!"

"To the bottom!"

Hands. A sea of hands. They were picking up the chant now, raising a racket that could no doubt be heard in port.

Jack let out a whoop of delight, then lent his voice to the chant.

And beside him, Elias Barth was laughing — laughing!

It was a sound Jack had never heard from the man.

On landing Jack was swarmed by sailors. After two sailors from New York left, he chose two replacements: a sharp-eyed, rugged Argentine named Luis Rivera and a Masai warrior-turned-sailor from British East Africa who called himself Robert.

In a drydock nearby, under repair, was a formidable-looking ship called the *Meriwether Lewis*. She was a barque, a three-masted vessel similar to the *Mystery* but with two full-rigged masts (fore and main) instead of one. Like the *Mystery*, she'd been fitted for an engine. Which meant she, too, was heading into treacherous waters.

As Jack checked the men's papers and gave them their orders, the barque's captain walked over to introduce himself. His name was Lawrence Chapman Walden and he was an American cartographer, attempting to be the first man to map every inch of Antarctica's coastline.

"Greenheart, eh?" Walden said, glancing at the *Mystery*. "Guess you're heading my way. South Pole attempt?"

"Well — I —" Jack stammered.

"Don't worry, your secret's safe with me." Walden grinned. "Must be a secret if I don't know about it. The government's keeping mine quiet, too. They're worried I'm going to fail, I guess. That'd be bad publicity for Uncle Sam. When you leaving?"

"As soon as we can load up — you?"

"A few more weeks." Walden wrote quickly on a sheet of white paper. "Here's our plan, more or less. Maybe we'll run into each other at one of the hotels."

Jack laughed. As he took the sheet, Walden

pulled a tiny American flag out of his pocket. "Here, you take something of mine and give me something of yours. It'll bring us both good luck. Old family superstition. Just do me one favor — leave the flag at the Pole, OK?"

"You bet," Jack agreed.

He was searching his pockets for a similar good-luck charm when the dogs arrived.

They came jumping off the back of a tumble-down slatted truck, thirty-five of them, flea-bitten and mangy, slavering and frustrated and cabin-crazy. Their ears were chewed, their mouths frothing as they ran among the sailors, jumping and barking.

"They have to be kidding," Jack murmured. "Excuse me, Captain Walden."

"Chappy," Walden corrected. "And bon voy-age!"

Jack ran to the truck. "Who brought these?" he demanded.

A dark, bushy-mustached man lumbered over to him. He wore a dark blue wool cap and gestured toward the dogs as he spoke. "Dogs is no have food!"

"These can't be the ones I asked for," Jack said. "I was assured they were the best. Who are you?"

"Kosta, Greek, me. Work Argentina, drive

truck. English no good. Man have truck. Give to me dogs. Dogs is good."

"What's he talking about?" Andrew asked.

"The dogs came in shifts from the north," Jack said. "A relay. Trucks were to wait at each touch point, give the dogs rest and food."

Kosta shook his head. "No food. Man say no *leptà* — money. Me have no money."

"Oh!" shouted Philip's voice. "Get that beast off my leg! I'm allergic to dogs!"

"O *popopo* . . ." Kosta disappeared among the men.

Jack and Andrew took chase. They saw Kosta kneeling on the dock, his arms wrapped around an Alaskan husky, whispering Greek into its ear. Philip was backing away, sneezing.

The dog whimpered, its head slumped and sheepish. "This Socrates. Is love peoples." Kosta turned around and beckoned, "Plutarchos! Taki! Dimitriou!"

The dogs came running. They gathered around him, pawing the ground pathetically as he soothed them.

Mansfield, the second in command, slid through the crowd toward Jack. "Bad news, Pop. The dog handler bailed out. Says Putney reneged on the agreed salary."

Jack saw red. The trip was in full swing, and Horace was penny-pinching. All along, he had scoffed at Jack's budget for the dogs. They were animals, he'd said. They could live on nothing.

"What about the dog food?" Jack asked. "All those tons of whale meat? The dogs can't eat only pemmican and hardtack."

Mansfield smiled. "Folded the meat into the general-storage budget. The butcher's gone back for it. He brought good Argentine steaks for the men and we put them in the hold, but —"

"Then unload some of them, on the double."

"Yes, sir!"

Kosta's face brightened. "*Ah, bravo, paithàkia mou! Thah fatteh crèas!*"

The dogs began leaping all over Kosta, barking excitedly.

"They understand that?" Andrew asked.

The dogs watched the ship expectantly until Mansfield came down the gangplank with an armful of wrapped steaks. "Come 'n' get it!"

The dogs bolted.

Mansfield was a goner.

"No!" Jack yelled.

"*KATHISETEH!*" Kosta's voice boomed out over the dock.

The dogs stopped reluctantly. One by one, they looked over their shoulders at Kosta, whining, as their hindquarters sank to the ground.

Jack had an idea.

"Kosta," he said, "do you by any chance mind the cold?" He pantomimed a shiver and gestured toward the ship and then south.

"Krio?" Kosta asked, mirroring the shiver. He looked out to sea. *"Ochi Antarktikos?"*

"Yes!" Jack exclaimed. "Antarcticos, that's it!"

Kosta thought for a moment. "Me no have money."

"I'll give you free room and board. And money, yes, after we return — if I have to take it out of my own account."

"Money, yes?" Kosta smiled. "Is good. Kosta love dogs."

Jack extended his hand. "Welcome aboard."

A list of the crew of the *Mystery*, as of September 5, 1909:

Jack Winslow — expedition leader
Elias Barth — captain
Peter Mansfield — second in command and chief navigator
John Siegal — first mate
Luis Rivera — second mate
Colin Winslow and *Andrew Douglas Winslow* — junior officers
Dr. Ross Montfort — general physician
Dr. Harold Riesman — veterinarian
Dr. Frank Nesbit — biologist
Dr. David Shreve — geologist
Harv Talmadge — meteorologist
Jacques Petard — physical instructor and chaplain
David Ruskey — photographer
Kosta Kontonikolaos — dog handler
Sam Bailey, *Pete Hayes*, *Vincent Lombardo*, *Mike Sanders*, *Chris Ruppenthal*, *Bruce Cranston*, *George Oppenheim*, *James Windham*, *Robert* (last name unknown) — able seamen
Tim O'Malley — able seaman/second cook
Hank Brillman — electrician

Wyman Kennedy — carpenter
Horst Flummerfelt — machinist
Rick Stimson — cook
Philip Westfall — helpmeet at large
Aspros, *Chionni*, *Demosthenes*, *Dimitriou*, *Eleni*, *Fotis*, *Galactobouriko*, *Hera*, *Hercules*, *Iosif*, *Ireni*, *Kalliope*, *Kristina*, *Kukla*, *Loukoumada*, *Maria*, *Martha*, *Megalamatia*, *Michalaki*, *Nikola*, *Panagiotis*, *Pericles*, *Plato*, *Plutarchos*, *Skylaki*, *Socrates*, *Sounion*, *Stavros*, *Taki*, *Taso*, *Tsitsifies*, *Vrochi*, *Yanni*, *Yiorgos*, *Zeus* — dogs

6

Colin

October 16, 1909

"We're shipping water like crazy! Don't let it rise to the engine! Bail!"

Kennedy was screaming.

There had to be almost a foot of water now. Colin dug two five-gallon buckets into it and pitched the water out the bilge hole. He'd been doing it for an hour now, along with another sailor, a hulk of a man named Flummerfelt.

"If this isn't bailing, I don't know what is!" Colin shouted back.

Colin's biceps ached. His calves ached. The ship was pitched upward, maybe forty-five degrees. It was like climbing a mountainside in a flash flood.

His clothes clung to him, soaking wet. He'd spent as much time slipping into the water as walking through it.

Father had warned about the Drake Passage. The gulf of storms. The only sea that wrapped itself around the entire planet — no interruption by land, nothing to tame it. When the sea swelled, it swelled for miles. Winds were sudden and violent. The Drake Passage had no limits, no rules, no pity.

The *Mystery* was tossing like a toy. Although her sides were tight, the water was pouring in over the bulwarks and onto the decks. The engine room was the lowest point, and if the water rose any more, it would wreak havoc with the machinery.

Colin planted his feet carefully and walked to the bilge hole. Through the hatch above them came the stench of sweat, vomit, and wet canine. The dogs had been brought belowdecks with the crew, and their frightened howls vied with shouts and the occasional guttural choke of a sailor who hadn't made it to the head in time.

Only Kennedy, Colin, and Flummerfelt were in the engine room.

Colin was "carpenter's apprentice" these days, which meant he was always with Kennedy. This was

Father's latest plan. It was supposed to get Colin to work hard, bring him "out of his shell."

It was ridiculous. Colin understood little about woodworking. Or Southerners with rancid senses of humor.

"What are you doing, Flummerfelt, drinking the water?" Kennedy shouted. "And Winslow, get in here before I grow gills!"

Colin rushed back. Kennedy was lying in the water, tinkering with the bilge pump.

"Doesn't it waste more time fixing that" — Colin stooped and filled the buckets again — "than it would if you bailed, too?"

Kennedy threw a bucket at him. "Who made you captain?"

Colin doubled his effort. Soon the pump was working, and Kennedy helped bail. As the water level began to drop, Jack poked his head into the room. "Where's your brother?"

"How should I know?" Colin replied. "And he's not my brother!"

"Find him! Make sure he's all right!" Jack said, rushing back to the bow.

Colin dropped his buckets. Make sure *Andrew* was all right. Andrew was a big boy. Couldn't he take care of himself?

Colin left the engine room and elbowed his way through the cabin. He lifted the steerage hatch and called down. No answer.

As he stood up, Socrates jumped on him, wagging his tail and yelping. With Kosta's care and a steady diet of whale meat, the dogs had put on weight.

"*Katto!*" Kosta commanded.

Socrates sat, and Colin took his paw. The dog's face was ringed with wet fur that stood straight up. He looked like a big, smiling hedgehog. "You didn't eat Andrew, did you?" Colin asked.

"Andrew?" Kosta said. "He go opp-stairs!"

"He's on deck? In *this*?"

Kosta nodded. "*Neh, neh.*"

Colin raced up the ladder. The rain hit him like an open hand. He struggled to open his eyes against it.

Andrew was alone, at the foremast, fumbling with the halyards. The sail was flapping violently.

"Heave to!" Colin shouted. "Cut the line and heave —"

He had to shut his mouth. He was swallowing water. In this rain, you could drown standing up.

Leaning into the wind, Colin struggled toward the bow, around the battened-down mountain of coal. Before them the water rose, black and steep, like a giant endless hill. For purchase he dug the sides of his boots into the empty kennels, which were bolted to the inside of the hull.

The main and mizzenmasts were safely lashed. Bailey and Hayes had taken care of that.

But Andrew was pulling on the halyards. Tightening the foresail.

"Take it down! Heave to!" Colin lunged forward and grabbed his stepbrother's shoulder. "What are you doing?"

"You said 'Heave ho!'" Andrew shouted.

"Heave *to*, you fool!" Colin grabbed the halyards and released them from their catches. They shot upward through the winches, and as the sail slackened it gave a gunshot of a snap.

Colin quickly gathered in the sheets. The sail was sodden, heavy with the weight of water, but Andrew just stood there. "Help me!" Colin cried out.

Andrew tried to put his arms around the sail, but the boom swung sharply, knocking him to the deck and pulling Colin with it.

Colin tried to hold fast. But his hands were frozen and wet, his fingers losing their feeling. The sail slipped out of his grip and billowed out behind him. He tried to haul it back in, but the wind caught it, suddenly snapping it outward.

The halyards ripped through their pulleys and the sail flew away, waving like a lost ghost over the side of the ship.

"Look what you did!" Colin shouted.

"I didn't do it!"

They were yelling now, yelling at each other across the boom as Colin struggled with numb fingers to fasten it.

"Why were you up here?" Colin demanded. "You don't know how to handle the foremast!"

"I read all about it!" Andrew shouted.

"You can't learn this stuff in books!"

"Colin, there are plenty of spare sails in the gallows."

"And with you here, we're sure to use every last one!"

"If you're so smart, why weren't you up here?"

"I was bailing!"

"Why?"

"What do you mean, why?"

"If you're such a good sailor, you shouldn't be bailing. You should be doing the hard jobs, like this one."

"There are plenty of fools here who want to do this."

"And you don't?"

"You want to argue? Here?"

Colin went for the hatch, but Andrew pulled him back. "Why are you dogging it? Why are you letting your shipmates down? To prove a point?"

"I'm not trying to prove anything!"

"You're trying to sabotage your own father's trip, because you didn't want to go!"

"And you did. You were dying to. You thought this was one big storybook adventure. Andrew of the High Seas. Your mother wasn't even cold in her grave, you heartless little —"

Andrew lunged at him but fell to the deck as Colin ducked away.

Colin tried to keep upright on the slick surface but went down hard. Both of them slid toward the stern, hydroplaning on the water until they crashed against the stern bulkhead.

Colin leaped to his feet. He'd had enough. He hadn't asked to be in the same family as Andrew. He'd never liked Andrew.

He threw a punch. Andrew scrambled away, kicking out with his leg and clipping Colin's ankle.

As Colin fell to the deck, he spotted a light glowing in the center of the deck. The hatch was open and Bailey peered out.

"Fight!" he cried.

"Fight!" "Fight!" "Fiiiight!"

The men were filing out of the hatch now, into the storm.

"Five to one odds on Colin!" Lombardo called out.

Hayes piped up, "I give the little guy two to one!"

"Show me the money!"

Like spectators at a cockfight. That's how they saw this. They dug into their pockets, leaning into the wind and rain, pulling out coins and bills.

"Come on," Andrew said. "Take the first punch. Get yourself locked up in the brig, Colin. That's what you want, isn't it? An excuse to do absolutely nothing!"

That did it. Andrew had stepped over the line.

Colin reared back and prepared to knock his head to Elephant Island.

7

Philip

October 16, 1909

Let them kill each other, Philip thought. They both deserve it.

Above him, the men were throwing money around. Thirsting for blood. The Romans. Friday night at the Colosseum. Gladiator against lion. Man against beast. Civilization against chaos.

That's what it always boiled down to, didn't it? That was what this trip was all about. What life was about.

Soon they would all be beasts. Every last one.

Chaos always won out.

"Stop this nonsense!"

Ah, the intrepid leader, Winslow the Wise.

Still dedicated to the cause, despite the slow breaking apart of his own family.

Winslow ran onto the deck, slipping in the water. He pulled Colin back, wrestling him to the deck.

A few punches had been thrown, all misses.

Pity.

Philip sank back down into the cabin. It was dry there. No use wasting a good warm space during a storm.

The dogs were making a racket, yipping restlessly at the commotion above. A few of the sailors remained, playing cards, recovering from their seasickness.

Philip hadn't enjoyed the motion much himself. The close quarters and the smell hadn't helped matters, either. He'd been bedridden through the whole storm.

If "bed" was the correct word for that minuscule wooden box lined with horsehair.

As Philip walked unsteadily across the sloped floor, Ruskey looked up from a game of cards. "Deal you in?" he asked.

"Not for that," Philip replied.

Ruskey smiled. He caught the hint.

Philip had already slipped him a good bit of

change. British, of course, but it could be cashed at any U.S. bank. Then it would make its way into the system, eventually returning to its country of origin, where its history might or might not be discovered, but by then it wouldn't matter. No one could trace money that closely.

Philip changed into his nightshirt and removed his shoes, then crawled into his bunk and pulled a ratty blanket up to his chin. They'd placed him where he had minimal contact with the other sailors, near the steerage hatch. The indignity of it all.

Quietly he slipped his hand under the bed and slid out his steamer trunk. Pulling it open, he reached under his clothing and flipped up a false bottom.

He pushed aside the newspaper clippings. At this angle, his fingers could just riffle through the pile of money. It felt comforting. He would sleep easier tonight, despite the storm.

He shut the trunk, locked it, and slid it back into place.

The storm seemed to be subsiding now. The weather was like that in the Drake Passage. Easy come, easy go. The men above deck were still noisy, but their utterances sounded happy, relieved.

Philip's appetite was returning. He eyed the steerage hatch. Below was the food storage. A hundred pounds of chocolate reserved for special occasions.

He'd already helped himself on a couple of sleepless nights. Tonight seemed perfect for another visit. To celebrate surviving the storm, of course.

Philip climbed out of bed, put on his glove-leather slippers, and took a small kerosene lamp from a shelf. Then he tiptoed to the hatch, pulled it open, and descended.

A dim light still shone from the bow, where the engine room was. Philip listened to hear if Kennedy had returned, but apparently he had not.

In the dim lamplight, the sacks looked like carcasses. He stepped closer and read the labels: RICE, FLOUR, MEAT . . .

A sudden noise made him jump.

A rat, Philip thought.

He held his breath and listened carefully. Now he could hear a scraping sound.

It was larger than a rat.

And it was coming from around the next corner.

"Hello?" Philip squeaked.

He peered around the corner, thrusting his lamp into the darkness.

Something moved. A barrel top.

Philip retreated. He doused his light and clung to the wall. To his right was a supply closet. He tried the knob and slowly pulled it open.

Its shelves were packed with cleaning fluids, but the floor had adequate space. He ducked in and closed the door.

Footsteps now. Walking past the closet.

A sailor. Brillman, maybe. Sanders. Sneaking down for a little nip of the spirits.

The steps faded, then stopped. Philip counted to 243 and then pushed the door open.

The lights were out. The place was pitch-dark.

He crept out into the hold and shut the door behind him.

Shiiiishhh.

A match. Where?

Philip spun around.

The light flared. He made out a face.

He opened his mouth to scream, but a hand closed over it. It wrenched him around, held him tight against a short body.

"Not a word," a voice said.

It was a British accent. Lower class.

Philip tried to speak, but the hand closed tighter. "I want up."

"Oob?" Philip said.

The man released his hand. "I'm a sailor. I ain't got me papers, but I can work. An' I been dreamin' of the Souf Pole all me life."

A lunatic. A certified inmate of Bedlam. "Well, that's just lovely," Philip said. "What say we just go upstairs and meet the captain, and you'll tell him your little story, and he'll —"

"A countryman, eh?" The man was drawing the match closer to Philip's face. "You look familiar, too."

Philip backpedaled. "Odd. You don't. I daresay our paths have not crossed in the schools. Perhaps your family is in landscaping — private homes, London?"

"Yes. You're one of those yoofs, aren't you?"

"Yoofs?"

"Right, the yoofs who took 'at money from the bank — just walked right in an' 'anded the teller the note, an' 'em well-dressed and all, like proper gen'l'men. Ten fousand pounds it was."

"I'm sure I don't know what you're talking about."

"It was in all the newspapers. Pictures, too. Face just like yours."

He knew. He knew and he was *here*.

Of all the dumb luck.

"I — I didn't realize I had become such a celebrity," Philip said.

"Well, not 'ere, maybe. But all the 'oity-toity mums in London is takin' their sons to school in fear that you're on the loose."

"Lovely," Philip said. "No wonder Uncle wanted rid of me. He hates bad publicity."

"Uncle?"

"Look," Philip said. "There are certain things that must not be said, whether they are true or not, which I am not saying they are, you understand. . . ."

"I understand." The man grinned. "Now *you* understand this: You will tell the captain you brought me on board. We're old friends, like. You will take all the blame. An' you will get me a nice, big meal."

Philip nodded numbly. "Yes. Yes, of course. And you are . . . ?"

"Name's Nigel." The man stuck out his hand. "Pleased to make your acquittance."

8

Andrew

October 31, 1909

He was dreaming about his father, his real father back in Boston, but the face was coming in and out of focus. They were sitting near the riverbank, Papa, Mother, and Andrew, and the boat race was in full swing, the Head of the Charles. Three ladies with parasols walked by and one of them looked at Papa and gave him a smile — just like the smiles Mother used to give Papa, and Andrew didn't like that, because Mother didn't have those smiles anymore, and he asked, Who's she? but Papa answered, Nobody, Andrew, let's watch the race.

So Andrew was trying to watch the sculls on the river — they scared him because he thought they were made of real skulls — when he saw that Mother was crying and Papa was mad, and Andrew worried it would get bad like the week before, when Mother had to run to the police. So he tried to stop them and all of a sudden Papa turned toward him but he wasn't Papa anymore — his face had changed into a skull, grinning and chattering, and he lunged toward Andrew, yelling in a muffled voice, striking out with a fist, hitting Andrew in the jaw, and he had to scream. . . .

The yelling awakened Andrew.

It was real. Not a dream. Coming from above, from the deck. Captain Barth's voice.

Andrew sat up, gasping for air. Sweat soaked his nightshirt. The dream's image lingered in his mind.

He rubbed his jaw where it hurt. That was real, too, but it was Colin who'd done that damage, not Papa, not a skull.

Andrew had been thinking a lot about Papa lately. About whether Papa knew what had happened to Mother, whether he'd heard about this trip. Whether he cared.

The whole time Mother had been married to Jack — four years — Papa hadn't called once. Not once. When Mother died, Andrew had telephoned him twice through the Boston operator. He reached the butler each time and left messages, but you never knew with butlers.

Andrew hoped Papa would come to the funeral, but he hadn't. Nor had Gram and Gramps. They hadn't spoken to Mother since she'd left Papa for Jack. Just cut her off, as if she'd never been their daughter.

Andrew shook away the thoughts. No use dwelling on them. You can't control the past.

He pushed away the flimsy sheet that passed for a curtain across his bunk. Through a nearby porthole he could see hints of the dawn struggling to break through the thick sea mist. Dawn came early in this part of the world. Already they were approaching the Antarctic Circle, tilted toward the sun at such an angle that the darkness fell barely two or three hours. Mansfield, the second in command, had reported seeing chunks of ice in the water.

Andrew threw back his blanket and stood to see the wall clock. Ten after three. He'd been asleep two and a half hours.

Standing up made his jaw throb — but despite the pain, he felt grateful. The punch had only

note 2 Bureaucracy

A type of organization structured like a pyramid, with one person at the top and many at the bottom workers at each level supervise those below them

glanced him. Had Colin made full contact, the *Mystery* might have had its first casualty.

He peered into the bunk above him. Colin was still asleep. Just about everyone was asleep, it seemed. The cabin resounded with snores and wheezes, human and canine. On the floor, Kosta slept with the dogs. Next to him was Socrates, a protective paw draped over his rag doll. It was a funny-looking little man wearing a tall red hat with a long tassel, a short puffy white skirt, and shoes with pompons. His name was Evzonos; Kosta proudly claimed that his outfit was standard for Greek soldiers.

Which could explain why the Greeks were no longer a world power.

Andrew tried to doze, but Barth's yelling was too loud. The man was as good-humored as a porcupine. Hardly anyone was immune to his tongue-lashings, and he never seemed to sleep.

Andrew could make out some claptrap about an "egregious violation of the maritime code." Barth loved his maritime code. According to Kennedy, he slept with it under his pillow.

Colin peered down from his bunk. "Are you up?"

"I am now," Andrew replied.

"Who is that up there with Barth?"

"How should I know?" Andrew asked.

"You must know *something*."

"Last night you promised Pop you'd be decent to me."

"I was decent. I was just stating a fact. You must know something."

"You haven't lost any of your hateful qualities overnight."

"Thank you."

Colin pulled on some clothes, pulled open his bunk curtain sheet, and climbed out. Without a word to Andrew, he slid down and walked toward the hatch.

No use trying to sleep now. Andrew dressed and ascended the hatch stairs behind his stepbrother.

Jack was abovedecks, too. "I checked the stores," he said to Captain Barth. "It seems this young man has helped himself for quite a few days down there."

"In the old days we would throw people like you overboard," Barth growled. "As excess steerage."

Andrew closed the hatch behind him, gaping at the scene by the starboard railing.

Jack and Barth were facing two men. One was

Philip. But the other was a stranger, short and wiry, wearing loose, disheveled clothing. He had a ruddy, pugnacious face that didn't flinch under Barth's verbal assault.

"I assure you, sir," Philip said, "Nigel is my dear friend. He's quite . . . seaworthy and should prove a jolly companion to all —"

"I don't care if he's Horace Putney himself," Barth said. "I hold you accountable for smuggling him in, Westfall. So, Nigel, you want to be part of this voyage? Fine. Henceforth I permanently assign both of you to the following jobs: fetching the fresh water and ice, cleaning the engine, washing the latrine, cleaning up after the dogs —"

"Sir," Philip cut in, "if I may be so bold, none of my work experience qualifies me for such menial tasks —"

"Excellent, Westfall. Then you will learn something. Begin with the deck floors. You know where the supplies are."

"I fank you, sir," Nigel said, "for your kind understanding of me circumlocutions."

"Dismissed."

Philip looked as if he were going to cry. Before he could protest, Nigel grabbed his arm and pulled him toward the hatch.

"Andrew," Jack said, "at the first sign of the horizon, would you give the captain a reading? Colin, rouse the men and tell them to rig a new foresail — then let's raise the mainsail and see how she sets. Captain Barth, you and I will take stock of the damage to the stores."

"Aye, aye, sir," Andrew said.

Before leaving, Jack gave a sharp look to Colin, who turned away.

"'Aye, aye, sir,'" Colin sang softly in a mocking, high-pitched voice as he headed toward the hatch.

Do not rise to the bait, Andrew told himself.

He took the sextant, a logbook, and the navigator's map from the compass binnacle. Carefully he looked through the sextant lens. The view was split down the middle, one half circle looking straight ahead, the other reflecting an image from a moveable mirror. You were supposed to find the horizon on the one side and the sun on the other. Then, using a handle that swiveled along a U-shaped index arm, you brought the sun's image down to line up with the horizon. That gave you the angle of the sun, which you then matched to certain nautical tables to tell your exact latitude, longitude, and bearing. You compared that to your course and made adjustments.

Andrew had read all about it. Studied the technique. He felt confident he could do it.

But in the mist, he couldn't see the horizon line.

He looked away from the sextant, gazing out to sea, looking for someplace where the fog had burned off.

By now, the crew was waking, the smell of coffee and bacon wafting up from below.

"Look who's setting our course!" Hayes shouted from the hatch.

"Uh-oh, South Africa, here we come," said Oppenheim, a nervous fellow with a sarcastic edge.

"See any mermaids?" Lombardo asked.

Andrew ignored them. Slowly but surely, he would learn. He would learn it all, until he was the best navigator, the best seaman on board.

Then no one would mock him.

He stared through the viewfinder intently, finally seeing a slight shift in the quality of light across the left circle. It was the closest thing to a horizon he'd seen.

He lined up the sun with it, matched its angle

to the appropriate column in his nautical logbook, and wrote down the reading: Longitude 122° 14' W., latitude 65° 02' S. and heading west by southwest. Only two degrees north of the Antarctic Circle. A slight southward adjustment would put them back on the course outlined on the navigator's map.

Now about half the men were on deck, raising the sails, swabbing the decks, letting down dredge nets off the port bow. Ruskey leaned over the starboard hull, photographing a distant school of killer whales.

Andrew opened the binnacle to put away the sextant.

"If you're off by the slightest amount," Colin called out, "we're in big trouble."

Andrew held the sextant toward him. "Fine. You do it."

Colin grabbed it and casually looked through it. After a few quick shifts of the arm, he announced his reading.

Longitude 122° 14' W., latitude 65° 02' S., heading west by southwest.

"Thanks," Andrew said with a smile.

He turned away and headed for the hatch. Captain Barth was just below, barking orders to everyone.

"Sir," Andrew said, holding out his book, "our course readings."

Barth grabbed it abruptly and called into the cabin: "Mansfield, get off your duff and set your course by this, on the double!"

"Can I finish breakfast?" came Mansfield's voice.

"You should be done by now!"

His mouth full, Mansfield bounded up the ladder. As he passed Andrew, he muttered, "Knock him over the head with the sextant. He needs the sleep."

Andrew followed him to the wheelhouse. Colin was nearby, and he glanced at the book as Mansfield set it by the tiller, open to Andrew's reading.

"Hey, you wrote down my numbers," Colin said.

"They were the same as mine," Andrew replied.

"Liar."

"Decency, Colin," Andrew reminded him. "Remember what you promised Pop."

"He's not your pop." Colin turned away abruptly. "Don't try to compensate for what you don't have."

Andrew grabbed his shoulder and spun him around. "I beg your pardon?"

"You heard me."

"I have a father, Colin."

"Harding Douglas the Third? When was the last time you heard from him?"

"That's no business of yours."

"What kind of man breaks off contact with his own son for no good reason?"

"My mother left him — for your dad!"

"No, she didn't leave him. Not totally. She got stuck with his carbon copy."

Enough. That was enough. Andrew didn't care how big Colin was. He hauled back and threw a punch.

Colin ducked away, laughing. "Come on, Andrew, this time you land the first blow. See what Jack says to that."

Andrew reared back again — but he lost his balance. The ship gave a sudden lurch to port.

"Iceberg!" shouted Rivera.

"Head to starboard!" Lombardo boomed.

By the starboard railing, Robert was waving his arms frantically. "Man overboard!"

Ruskey was gone.

9

Elias Barth

October 31, 1909

Barth braced himself as the *Mystery* heeled hard. The iceberg passed to port, not 200 yards away. It had been a close call, yet only five men — Mansfield, Siegal, Rivera, Jack Winslow, Robert — were handling the maneuver. The rest were gathered at the starboard railing, everyone shouting instructions and no one doing a thing.

Fools, Barth thought. Every last one of them.

It was a ship of fools.

A man overboard, no doubt. And all they could do was yammer. Where was the discipline? Nowadays the men had shoddier character, pudding for brains.

Barth elbowed his way through them. "Throw him a line!" he cried out.

"He has one," Rivera replied.

The idiot photographer was hanging on a halyard, swinging over the water with one arm, holding his camera with the other.

"Pull him up!" Barth commanded.

"He won't come up," said Robert.

Ruskey's legs were wrapped around the halyard, bearing some of his weight. With his free hand, he was aiming the camera downward, snapping photographs of the ice-chunked water.

Photographs!

"Sailor, get up here right now!" Barth barked.

Ruskey was beaming. "This is absolutely remarkable!"

"I don't care!" Barth replied. "I can't afford to have you —"

With a loud crunch, the ship jolted again.

Ruskey lost his balance. His camera flew into the surf. He let go of the halyard, whirling his arms, screaming.

Barth lunged forward and grabbed the line. Ruskey hung from the end of it, suspended by the loops around his feet.

Barth pulled, but the halyard slipped. It had iced up.

Bodies jostled him from all sides. Total chaos. No organization whatsoever.

"Let me do it!" a voice cried out.

A pair of arms muscled Barth aside and grabbed the line from him.

It was Winslow's son, the big, lazy one. Colin. He wrapped the halyard around his right wrist and began to pull, yanking Ruskey upward as if he were a child.

Astonishing. The boy had the strength of a moose.

In a moment, Ruskey was sprawled on the deck, breathing in violent gasps. His eyes darted. He was obviously in shock — yet the crew just stood there, cheering. Brillman was taking off his shirt and threatening to retrieve the camera. Hayes was asking Ruskey if he'd kissed any fishies.

Idiots.

Dr. Montfort was at the edge of the crowd, blocked by the oblivious men. Barth shoved his way back through and pulled him toward Ruskey.

But Ruskey was sitting up and laughing now as the men slapped him on the back. As if they were in a beer hall. A saloon. Montfort could hardly get through them.

Ruskey would be punished as an example to the others. Calculated risks were part of a seaman's trade; careless behavior weakened the moral fiber of the crew.

They would need moral fiber in spades. This voyage was a war, really, fought on a hostile battlefield against an enemy whose face was blindingly white and whose weapons were wind and cold. It would require the best of every man.

Captain Barth watched Colin move away from the periphery of the group. "Bully job," he called out. "You saved his life."

Colin nodded tersely and walked away, back to the rigging.

Strong, heroic — but rude. The boy needed a lesson in manners.

The men were helping Ruskey toward the hatch now. He limped along painfully. Beyond them, the sun had burned off most of the mist.

Captain Barth narrowed his eyes. The surf looked white-capped, yet its motion was a gentle rolling. He grabbed a telescope from inside the binnacle and looked through.

Brash ice.

It was unmistakable — broken up bits of ice floes, bobbing on the sea. In the distance, he could hear a faint, high-pitched sound, like the moan of an old woman.

Mansfield had heard it, too. "What on earth is that, Captain?"

"The ice," Barth said.

It was exactly as Scott had written. As the edges of the floes scraped against one another, they made a noise that reverberated through the ice as a loud groan.

But where were they? It was hard to tell. The sound seemed to be coming from all over.

"How close are we?" Mansfield asked.

Barth grabbed the sextant and pointed it toward the horizon line. Taking a reading, he checked it against the course. "Head to starboard again, Mansfield! We're off by five degrees. At this rate we'll plow into an ice shelf before we reach the Ross Sea."

"Five degrees? Who set this course?"

It was the boy, Barth realized. Andrew. How stupid to have trusted him to take the reading.

"Just set her right! We're heading into Antarctica, my friend, dead or alive."

10

Colin

November 6, 1909

"Looks like we've got a nor'easter!" Bailey called from the foretop.

Colin was already at work, setting the mainsail, then helping Bailey trim the fore topsail against the freshening wind.

They were running before a high following sea and picking up good speed. The *Mystery* had been sailing due west-southwest for six days now, finally within the Antarctic Circle, tracing a semicircle parallel to the continent. Although the summer sun was out nearly all day, every day, today the mist obscured the light. Colin looked out at a leaden sea, mostly stream ice, easy enough to navigate.

He had seen it before, in the bays and inlets of the north: the freak weather conditions, the tricks that the light played on your perception, the way the ice sang as it froze. His mother would sing along with it as they sailed, somehow finding a strange melody that connected the drone of the ice to the call of the petrels. Here the music was deeper, fuller.

After a week of calm seas, the *Mystery* was rocking again. She wasn't built for comfort in storms. Her keel was rounded, like a bathtub, so that ice encroaching from the sides would slide underneath and simply lift her out of the sea. The shape had its disadvantages: The ship rode "soft," more susceptible to heeling and rocking. Everyone but Barth had experienced seasickness so far.

Colin had grown to love the ship. She was a wonder of construction, her hull reinforced with more than two feet of the sturdiest oak and Norwegian mountain fir. Her bow, where she would meet the ice, was twice as thick, constructed of specially chosen oak timbers whose natural curvature matched that of the ship's design. Breen had doubled the number of frames — the ribs of the ship — and doubled their thickness, too, to more than ten inches. The entire hull had been sheathed in a remarkable wood from a South American evergreen called greenheart, heavier than metal and tough enough to break ordinary tools.

The *Mystery* was as close to unbreakable — and iceproof — as they came.

Those qualities would come in handy soon. If all calculations were correct, they were approaching the eastern edge of the Ross Sea, where they'd tack and turn in.

Around them were abundant signs that they were near land. Terns, petrels, and fulmars screamed overhead. A giant albatross had landed on deck the day before, strutting imperiously. Killer whales had followed the *Mystery* for miles, maybe hoping for another try at Ruskey, and Nesbit, the biologist, claimed to have spotted crabeater seals on a distant ice floe.

As Colin secured the staysail halyard, he heard a sudden, bellowing whoosh of water to starboard.

Less than 100 yards due north, a blue-gray swell arose from the sea. It arced high, the water rolling off to reveal a leathery body, both fluid and impossibly massive, maybe 100 feet long.

A blue whale. The largest living thing on earth.

"Thar she blows!" Colin shouted.

The entire crew raced over to look. The geologist, Shreve, was bug-eyed, screaming for Ruskey to take photos.

"I didn't know they lived in waters this cold," Sanders remarked.

"Maybe that's why they're blue," Flummerfelt said.

"Where are the whaling ships?" asked Ruppenthal, a shrewd, tempestuous sailor with a head of flaming red hair.

"Around," Pop replied. "There are whaling stations in the Antarctic."

The dogs, who had been fast asleep in their kennels, now jumped to attention. But they headed in the opposite direction, toward port.

There, Kosta was clapping his hands and howling with glee. Not far away a group of pear-shaped, black-suited penguins were flopping onto the ice and sliding on their bellies.

Some of the men had gathered around Kosta, laughing and imitating the birds' peculiar sound.

Baart! Baart! Baart!

"Hey, Cap'n, they're calling you!" Lombardo shouted.

Captain Barth scowled. "Don't become too

fond of them. Someday soon they may be your breakfast, lunch, and dinner."

"I believe I am about to become sick," Philip muttered.

Nigel backed away. "Again?"

"Always looking on the bright side, eh, Cap'n?" said Talmadge, the balding, genial meteorologist.

"Back to your posts," Barth grumbled.

As the men returned to work, Lombardo began a sea chantey, in which Colin did not join. He kept his eye on the sea, which was changing rapidly as the *Mystery* neared its goal. The stream ice was breaking up into small but densely packed chunks, covered with patches of snow. The ice parted smoothly before the ship's prow, with the consistency of thick custard.

Colin could not stop thinking of Captain Barth's comment. Surely things would never become so dire that they'd have to eat penguins. Seals, perhaps. They didn't taste wonderful, but the meat was rich, and the blubber could be used as cooking fuel.

But penguins were not meant to be consumed. It would be as bad as eating the dogs.

Even the Norwegians wouldn't do that.

* * *

Colin had begun to doze off, standing up, when he felt a firm pat on his shoulder. "Why don't you go to sleep?"

At the sound of Father's voice, Colin tensed. "I was."

"I mean in your bunk. It's close to midnight."

The sky was dim but still sunlit. The sky was always sunlit, round the clock. Colin should have been used to it from his years of Alaskan summers, but he wasn't. At least there you had *some* darkness at night. Here, every day felt like a long three in the afternoon, followed by a couple of hours of near-sunset.

The sun was not visible through the mist, but the clouds were tinged red-orange. The temperature had dropped, and Colin felt an icy chill through his Burberry parka.

He was aware of a faint tinkly sound now, like the rustling of glass beads in a gentle breeze. It seemed to come from nowhere in particular, and yet it was everywhere at once, port, starboard, fore, and aft.

Then, in the dim twilight, Colin saw falling ice crystals, delicate gossamer needles, like wings shed by a million fairies. They winked and glistened, nestling finally in the pillowy pudding ice that surrounded the *Mystery*.

"What is this?" Colin asked.

"An ice shower, Colin. Frozen mist. The water particles crystallize and fall to the earth." Father's eyes were distant, moist. "I'd heard of these but never imagined they were as exquisite as this."

It was like nothing Colin had ever seen. Such fragile beauty in a landscape so harsh.

"Now are you happy you came?" Father asked.

Colin felt himself fold right up. "Happy?"

"Captain Barth says we've done two hundred miles today."

"Bully for Captain Barth."

"Bully for you, Colin. Your sailing skills helped make this possible."

"Only because you forced me to do more work."

"Oh. And here I thought you'd turned over a new leaf."

Colin didn't hear the comment. His attention had fixed on a dark shape emerging through the mist — an iceberg, far more massive than even the blue whale. "I — I think we're in trouble, Father."

"*Tack!*" he commanded. "*All hands on deck! Take her around hard!*"

Colin and his father scrambled for the mainsail sheet. Bailey and Sanders went for the mizzen, and Hayes and Lombardo trimmed the foresail. Captain

Barth flew out of the hatch, grabbing the sheet from Colin.

The ship heeled abruptly to starboard and Colin lost his balance. He slid along the ice-slicked deck, jamming his shoulder into the hull.

Without warning, the ice shower had thickened into a full-fledged storm, the crystals into hail-like pellets. Colin pulled his hood over his head and headed back to the mainsail. Father and Captain Barth had already been joined by two more sailors — and Andrew.

The *Mystery* was heading due south now. She'd been sailing in a strong crosswind and in a small amount of time had come close to another iceberg. It was at least a hundred feet tall, dense with snow and pocked with deep hummocks.

The ship was going to make it. Father had called it just in time.

The ice around the *Mystery* was changing now. No longer a soupy slush, it rammed the ship's hull in thick, odd-shaped chunks.

Through the pounding storm, Colin heard a deep, violent groan directly ahead of them, like the sound of an iron wall being torn open. The rumble could be felt through the planks of the decking.

All the sails were now set. Colin couldn't climb

the mast, so he leaped on top of the deckhouse. Shielding his eyes, he looked into the distance beyond the bow. From this vantage, he could see movement — an upward thrust, like a giant fist emerging from the ice.

Pressure. He had learned about this from Father. It happened close to the land, wherever there was pack ice — giant ice islands that traveled with the currents until they collided. The force would cause the floes to tent upward, pushing inexorably against each other until one finally gave. A high, jagged pressure ridge formed where one floe pushed over the top of the other.

It was no place for a wooden ship, even one clad in greenheart.

"Look at this!" Colin called out.

Barth climbed up beside him, squinting out over the pack ice. "Come about slowly, men!" he shouted.

Both of them hopped off and helped the crew slacken the sails. The *Mystery* edged slowly forward. Its prow was cutting through solid ice now, ripping it apart easily.

Father looked concerned. "It's young ice," he remarked. "Soft and thin. We're probably safe here for a while, but I don't want to head into the pack until the weather clears."

"Agreed," Captain Barth replied. He turned to amidships and shouted, "Heave to, men!"

"Are we stuck?" Colin asked.

"Don't ask that," Captain Barth snapped. "Don't ever ask that."

"Elias, it's a legitimate question," Father said.

"Negativity lowers morale," Barth replied, glowering at Colin. "I gave the command to heave to, Master Winslow."

Colin met his imperious glance but didn't move.

"Colin, help out," Father said.

Help out? What had he been doing? Who saw the iceberg and the pressure ridge first?

"Aye. Aye. Sir," Colin replied and turned away.

He had no use for either of them.

11

Philip

November 7, 1909

The ship was iced in. Iced in, for goodness' sake, and they hadn't even reached land, or reached ice, or whatever they called it.

No one was admitting the predicament. They called it "young" ice. Which was not as dangerous as old ice, presumably — although how you told the difference was beyond Philip. At any rate, they were all crowded in the hold, officers and sailors. Since the ship had hove to, there really wasn't much to do, which was just fine. Working side by side with Nigel had little appeal, and now, at least, Philip could do what he liked best, lying prone.

Everyone was playing. At the long table in the

center of the hold, Drs. Montfort and Riesman, the people doctor and the veterinarian, brooded over a game of chess, oblivious to the loud poker game next to them.

Jacques Petard, the trim and pious physical instructor/chaplain, had brought a phonograph. He was playing music of the vile, syrupy Gabriel Fauré, while the Greek sat to the side and wept, no doubt reminded of the howl of some beloved long-lost sheepdog.

Closer to Philip's bunk, Lombardo entertained with stories of his boyhood in Sorrento.

"And, of course, this part I will not go into on account of the age of some of the individuals present," Lombardo said for about the twentieth time, "but I'm sure the grown-ups among you will catch my drift."

As always, Philip understood exactly what he was saying, and, as always, it was a ridiculous, overinflated story of romance with some young *signorina* who in reality would never have the slightest thing to do with the likes of Lombardo.

"Thank you, Mr. Lombardo, for protecting my innocence," Philip said.

"I don't care about you, it's out of respect for Pop's sons," Lombardo said.

"And also, no doubt, out of respect for truth."

Lombardo bolted to his feet. "Why, you little —"

Philip was gone before he could finish the sentence.

The next morning Philip awoke cramped, sore, and itchy. He was certainly allergic to the horsehair on the bed, but Captain Barth had ignored his pleas for different padding.

His stomach, however, which had been perpetually upset over the last few weeks, now felt calm. It took a moment for him to figure out why.

The ship was still. Not moving, not swaying or listing or heeling or whatever they called it. It was as if it had suddenly run aground.

Just as he feared, they were locked in the ice.

Already the troops were bustling about. Stimson, the cook, was grilling bacon and eggs and percolating the tarlike sludge he called coffee. Philip pulled on his clothing, called out a cheerful good-morning that was not answered, and celebrated his calm tummy with a large heap of scrambled eggs. Flummerfelt barreled past him, taking two buckets of coal from abovedecks to the engine room.

Nigel was sitting at the table, swilling the coffee. "Eat up," he said. "We have pick duty."

"Pick duty?"

"Unless you want to use a saw."

"What on earth are you babbling about?"

The relative silence was broken by a monstrous *GRRRROMMMM* as the ship jerked forward. Nigel's coffee flew across the table, landing on Philip's lap.

"Blasted fool!" Philip said, bolting upward. "This is my only decent pair of trousers!"

"It was a decent cup of coffee, too."

"If you two are finished dining," Captain Barth said acidly, "perhaps you can join us abovedecks before the crème brûlée is served."

Such a sarcastic soul.

"Captain," Philip said, "begging your pardon, but you see, my trousers are wet from coffee and I must —"

"Not my problem, Westfall. In case you haven't noticed, the engines have been turned on — and I am ordering you both abovedecks to help free the *Mystery*."

"Aye, aye, sir!" Nigel piped up, clearing his plate and scampering upstairs.

As Captain Barth lumbered up after Nigel, Philip returned his plate to the sink. He grabbed a pile of dry dish towels, shoved them into his trousers to sop up the coffee, and went to get his pea coat and overcoat.

Moments later, Philip was sliding down a canvas chute that had been draped over the side of the ship. At the bottom, Andrew handed him a large instrument that resembled an overgrown hammer whose head tapered to blunt points at either end.

"What am I expected to do with this?" Philip asked.

"It's a pick," Andrew replied. "To chop the ice."

He gestured toward the bow of the ship. Three men, including Nigel, were already hacking away. Two others were using an outsized saw. The *Mystery*, despite the great sound of its engine, was barely moving.

Philip followed Andrew to the bow. He stood over a solid section of ice, lifted the pick over his head, and fell backward.

Nigel burst out laughing. "You're a fine sight better at robbin' banks, ain't you?"

The loudmouth. The simpleminded, lower-class twit.

Philip glared at Nigel, but no one seemed to have heard the comment. They were laughing, too, and Philip smiled tolerantly until they got back to work.

He began to chop at the ice, imitating Nigel. Soon his back hurt. His arms screamed with pain. The sun beat down, making the frigid weather seem downright balmy.

But before long, the *Mystery* picked up momentum and was blasting through the ice as if it were glass.

Part Three

Arrival

12

Andrew

November 11, 1909

"Steady as she goes . . ."

Jack spoke the command almost to himself. Already the *Mystery* was traveling at little more than a float. The entire crew was awake — standing at the port railing, wearing dark goggles, not saying a word.

The coast of Antarctica rose out of the sea, sheer and blinding. It towered over the ship and stretched in both directions like the rampart of a great ice city. Parts of the wall had fallen away, exposing bright blues and greens like broken quartz.

Someday, if they survived, they would find a way to describe this. But now all they could do was gawk.

"Shelf ice," Jack said. "The edge of the slab that covers the continent. It keeps slowly pushing out to sea, under the pressure of its own weight. Eventually it breaks off and calves part of itself into the sea."

"Icebergs," Sanders remarked.

"The colors show where the shelf split," Shreve explained.

Robert squinted intently. "Looks like emeralds are inside it."

"Sapphires," said Windham.

Shreve shook his head. "Ice looks white because of the air bubbles trapped inside it. What you see now is compressed ice. The air has been squeezed out — you're looking right through to the algae trapped inside. The green and blue."

"Algae," Philip said. "How poetic."

"It's like a bloody fortress," Nigel said. "'Ow are we supposed to get in — climb?"

No one answered.

The *Mystery* — its square- and gaff-rigged sails, its small city of men, its thick hide — seemed tiny and fragile. One swipe of an iceberg and it would all be splinters and bone.

Anchoring the ship looked impossible. Nothing remotely resembled an inlet here.

Andrew thought of what lay over the wall. Ice

mountains and snow gullies, deep crevasses, and long, sharp ridges of ice called *sastrugi*, shaped like the waves of the sea. Back home, it had seemed so exciting.

Now he wasn't sure.

Jack and Captain Barth had been huddling in the deckhouse for a long time. Through the window Andrew saw them gesturing over a pad of paper covered with cross-outs.

They were choosing teams. One to stay with the ship, the other to trek to the South Pole. Divide and conquer. If one group didn't survive, the other could bring news home.

No one knew who would be chosen. Jack had not made up his mind until now. That had been part of his plan.

Smart decision, Andrew realized. Teams meant sides. Haves and have-nots. The men who hadn't been chosen for the South Pole might resent those who had. Morale would have been destroyed.

Jack knew what he was doing.

Andrew envied the men who would be chosen. Surely Lombardo, for his toughness. Siegal, for his quick wits. Kosta, to tend the dogs.

He wished he were older. He wished, in a way, that the men would fail — not die, not be hurt, just *not make it*. Follow the wrong path, realize they didn't have enough food, something. Maybe Scott and Amundsen would fail, too. The South Pole would remain unclaimed until, oh, maybe 1914 or so, when Andrew would be old enough for consideration.

The morning passed slowly as the *Mystery* meandered along the coast. A southwesterly wind had blown much of the pack ice out to sea, and the weather was clear enough to plot a safe course through the leads.

Just before the lunch hour, Jack and Captain Barth emerged. Mansfield immediately blew the meeting whistle. The men filed onto the deck, and Jack began his speech.

Both of the groups, he said, would be equally important. The trekkers faced greater glory, but they risked their lives. The men remaining aboard the *Mystery* had a solemn responsibility; without them the trip could not succeed. They could enjoy day expeditions safely close to the ship.

Andrew glanced around him. The faces told a story. Everyone knew the trekkers would have the better deal.

"I will lead the Pole exploration," Jack announced. "And I will need the following thirteen men . . ."

Kosta. Of course.

Petard, for his skiing expertise.

Dr. Riesman, the vet.

Dr. Shreve, the geologist.

Ruskey, the photographer.

O'Malley, who could cook.

The sailors Siegal, Lombardo, Rivera, Ruppenthal, Cranston, and Oppenheim.

"What about Barth?" shouted Hayes.

Jack looked up from his list. "The captain will be in charge of those who remain on the *Mystery*."

Kennedy howled, falling to his knees. "Please, let me go with you!"

Some of the men laughed — mainly the ones who didn't have to stay; the others weren't so amused.

Andrew didn't blame them. Without Jack, Captain Barth would be hard to take.

Without Jack, Colin would be impossible.

"Andrew," Jack called out.

"Yes?" Andrew answered.

Jack looked at him quizzically. "You're going."

"Going where?"

"You're the thirteenth name," Jack said. "You're going to the South Pole."

Calm. He had to stay calm. This was a misunderstanding. A mental trick. Brought on by fatigue. It couldn't be true. It wasn't. The look on his father's face was steady, but it would break when he realized what he'd said.

"Unless," Jack said with a shrug, "you don't want to."

Now everyone was looking at Andrew, bewildered, expectant, waiting for a reaction, waiting to hear what on earth a sixteen-year-old would say upon learning he would be among the first people since the dawn of time to set foot on the South Pole.

And a sound burst forth, a bellow so loud and sudden and overwhelming that it took Andrew a moment to realize that it was coming from himself.

The next morning Andrew was jolted awake by the sound of Captain Barth's voice.

The men were racing about the cabin, the dogs yowling.

"Drop anchor! All hands on deck!"

Anchor. They were dropping anchor. That meant they'd found a port.

If they found a port, it was time to leave.

To the South Pole.

The South Pole!

Andrew leaped out of bed. He pulled on his clothes and raced above deck.

The *Mystery* had jibed south, directly into a cove. Here, at the base of a sloping ice shelf, was a shoreline. Not much, really: a few acres of gray-black rocks, covered with snow and guano — and a squadron of curious seals that one by one slid into the water as the ship approached.

"Lower the lifeboats and load 'em on out!" shouted Captain Barth.

The ship flew into motion. Bailey, Hayes, and Sanders pulled halyards, releasing the lifeboats. Andrew fell into a conveyor line hauling up supplies from the galley and the stores — whale meat and pemmican for the dogs, chops and canned food for the men. A large stove and two small wire Primus stoves. Coal, wood, matches, lanterns. Skis and snowshoes. Extra dry clothing, extra traces for the dogs. Medical supplies. Books. Three sledges and grease for the sledge treads. Photography and film equipment. Picks, saws, shovels, and a microscope. Clubs and rifles for hunting.

All of it had to be slid down canvas chutes into the four lifeboats. There wasn't enough room for anything else, so Lombardo, Hayes, Rivera, and

Ruppenthal boarded the boats by themselves and rowed them to shore. There they would unload, then return to pick up the men and dogs.

The two teams shared a giddy tangle of embraces, backslaps, and handshakes.

"Good luck, men," Captain Barth said. "I envy you."

Kennedy threw him a dubious glance. "So do we."

Colin had wandered to the other end of the ship. He was examining the rigging as Andrew approached him.

"Well . . ." Andrew began.

"Yeah," Colin mumbled.

"Don't leave without us, okay?"

Colin smiled wanly. "It's not in the plan."

Andrew extended his hand and his stepbrother took it.

"Bon voyage," Colin said.

"No hard feelings — about me going?"

"Nope. I wanted to stay."

Andrew nodded.

The lifeboats were returning now, and soon everyone — men and dogs — was sliding down the chutes. Somehow Lombardo ended up in the water, but Andrew believed he did it on purpose. To keep them laughing to the last possible minute.

As they sailed to shore, a wet snow began to fall. It clung to the oars and their clothing, and when Andrew looked back, the *Mystery*'s rigging was a glistening white web.

Andrew's boat was called the *Horace Putney*, and it had the appropriate size of its namesake, if not the luxurious trimmings. When it bottomed out on rocks close to the shore, they all climbed out into the shallows.

Andrew's knees buckled. He felt a brief wave of nausea.

"Lord, I'd forgotten what terra firma felt like," O'Malley said.

Andrew tried to walk, but his legs had a life of their own, as if he'd never stepped on solid land in his life.

But that's where he was — solid land. The land at the bottom of the world. Where no one had stood before. Ever.

The dogs tore off like a shot. Barking giddily, they dived into snowdrifts, rolled on rocks, ran in circles, and yapped at the seals, which were now watching from a safe distance.

"Socrates! Plutarchos! Taki!" Kosta shouted. "*Ella tho!*"

Ella tho. Come here. Andrew was beginning to pick up some of this. He'd have to. The dogs seemed to obey Greek more than English.

Ruppenthal had fallen to his knees and was kissing the earth. Dr. Shreve danced a crazy-looking jig.

As the lifeboats returned, a musket shot echoed off the sea, then another, the *Mystery* sending the men a farewell salute.

Lombardo, whose clothing had nearly frozen solid, was changing into dry togs. The others went to work loading the sledges.

They'd packed too much onto the boats. No one had thought to measure the provisions against the capacity of the sledges. Fully loaded, the sledges were nearly six feet high.

This was it, then. These were to be their moveable homes for the next few weeks.

"The temperature is twenty-one degrees Fahrenheit," Jack said. "This is about as warm as it gets. If we time this right, we'll make it back before the summer is out. Are we ready?"

"READY!"

"Then let's go, boys!"

"Yeeaaaaaaa!"

POW!

Another shot from the *Mystery*. A cheer across the sea, echoing their own.

"Stay within each other's sight at all times," Jack said. "We will use tie lines during snowstorms. Go slowly and alert each other of depressions of snow that might mask crevasses. If your toes and fingers lose sensation, stop immediately and let me know — frostbite is to be avoided at all costs. And if you get lost in a storm, for God's sake, keep yourself awake. Sleep will set in and try to lull you out of your misery — it's called the polar sleep, and it is the precursor of death."

"Right!" Siegal exclaimed. The others piped up in agreement.

Jack then led a prayer. As he intoned the twenty-third psalm — *The Lord is my shepherd, I shall not want* — Andrew's heart was beating so hard he could see the motion through his coat.

He closed his eyes and tried to concentrate, but he couldn't.

All he could see was the face of his mother.

And she was smiling.

13

Nigel

November 14, 1909

Sweeping the storage hold. *The storage hold.* Of all the insulting, menial tasks.

Nigel drew his broom across the wooden planks, sending up a cloud of dust. "D'yer understand wha' this means? D'yer realize wha' they're doin' to us?"

The boy's back was to Nigel. He was leaning over a barrel, no doubt eating. Or daydreaming. Or both. The only things he could do well, the pampered brat. "Hmm?"

"It's storage, Philip. What'll they have us do next — put up a little festive buntin', 'old a little dance — perhaps invite a few of the more attractive seals?"

Now he was turning around, the lazy imbecile.

"My good man," Philip said, "what on earth are you talking about?"

"I'm talkin' about an attempt by the upper classes to depress the workin'man —"

"I am not," Philip said, "nor do I ever intend to be, a workingman."

"I can *see* that —"

"Nigel, we are in a quiet place. We're surrounded by food. Two feet of solid lumber insulate us from the outside. Where are the others? Outside, chopping ice. Count your blessings."

"Exactly wha' they want you to say, Philip! That's 'ow it works — they numb you. Wear you down. Convince you it's all right."

"Nigel, you are a stowaway. I am a runaway. I don't see that we have any leverage here."

Nigel slammed his broom on the floor. "Of course you don't. You fink like they do. You fink they're so bloody smart. Well, consider this. Wha' sort of animal 'ave they taken wif 'em?"

"Dogs."

"And wha' else?"

Philip considered this a moment. "More dogs?"

"Right! Now, wha' does that tell you? It tells you they're fools. Now, if you follow the finkin' of Robert Scott — the best bleedin' explorer wha' ever lived — you know you're supposed to take ponies. Why? Because they're built for 'eavy pullin'. Because one of 'em can pull wha' free or four dogs can pull — plus, they eat grain, so you don't have to worry about spoilin' meat."

"It's well below freezing out there. The meat is frozen."

"You're ignorin' my point. It's the stupidity of it. *Fink*, Philip. They split the crew into two teams, an' they don't tell us until the last minute — very bad for morale. The team wha' leaves, they don't 'ave the right animals. So they're doomed. They can't contact us. Wha' 'appens to us if they don't return?"

"We go home, I suppose."

"And 'ow long d'yer suppose they're goin' to wait before they decides to do that? Six monfs? A year? While we sit 'ere an' mop the floors an' scrub the water closet an' say yes sir no sir to Barf?"

"Unless we freeze to death first."

"Exac'ly!" At last. The light of understanding. "'Ow long do you fink these men will last under Barf?"

Philip laughed. "They hate him."

"They'll 'ang 'im, they will. String 'im up from

the riggin', like whale meat. Then who calls the shots? No one. They'll all be fightin' to take over — Mansfield, Hayes, Kennedy. We'll be lucky if they don't slit each other's froats!"

"Lovely, then. You and I can sail home together."

"They'll kill us, too! Unless we act first, Westfall."

"Act? What do you mean, *act*?"

Nigel leaned into Philip, lowering his voice. "I mean, we take the ship from Barf an' sail it 'ome now."

Philip stared back, uncomprehending, as if Nigel had just spoken in Swedish. "You're joking, of course."

"They ain't comin' back, Philip. All them blizzards an' winds an' crevasses an' such? Not to mention they ain't got enough food. An' if those don't get 'em, the yeti will."

"The *yeti*?"

" 'Uge, ugly, 'airy fing. Lives in the snow, 'ides in caves. Freezes your blood and eats you 'ole. I 'eard about 'em from the Sherpas in Nepal, back two or free years ago when I been there —"

"You can't possibly believe in —"

"Face it. Winslow, Lombardo, all of 'em — it's

a fool's mission. No one's ever done it in all of 'istory. You fink an amateur explorer, a Greek truck driver, a teenage boy, an' a few flunkies is goin' to succeed where Scott failed? We 'ave to take the *Mystery* before the weather takes us."

"You're insane. You're totally barmy. You think you and I are going to —"

"Not just me an' you. The others, too. I been doing some listenin', Philip. A few of these fellows is feelin' the same as me — what's the point in waitin' 'ere? This is *summer*, for goodness' sake, and it's freezin'. What's autumn like — or winter? Listen, Philip, to the picks an' saws out there. The ship's locked in. They're workin' to free it — for wha'? To stand still until it freezes again?"

"But — but this is mutiny, Nigel!"

"That's your name for it. I call it survival. We start slow-like. Plant the seeds, if you will. I can count at least four men will join us right away, I'm sure — free more I know will turn. So, we leave little 'ints 'ere an' there, an' before you know it, we'll be the majority."

"Fine. Try it. But don't cry to me when Barth banishes you to the penguins."

" 'Ave it your way, Philip. If you're not in, it's all right by me. But if you ain't one of us, you're one of 'em. An' when we're in control, we do the banishin'. I understand the brig is none too comfortable. An' when we arrive 'ome, there's plenty of press contacts'll be very interested to 'ear who you are."

"That's blackmail!"

Nigel shrugged. "That's reality. Of course, you could say yes. We'll take over the ship, 'ead back to a 'ero's welcome. We'll tell the newspapers that the South Pole party, poor fellows, they died for the love of their country, sniff sniff."

"How do I know you won't turn on me?"

"As far as I'm concerned, you were never on the ship, Philip. You 'ide out an' sneak away after we land. Your uncle, I'm sure, won't put up a fuss."

"And if he does?"

"We'll tell 'im you died, too. That'll get the authorities off your tail. You set up a new identity for yourself in Milwaukee or some blasted place."

"I couldn't!" Philip protested.

"All right, then," Nigel said. "New York."

Philip slumped against the barrel. "Let me think about it."

Nigel smiled.

14

Andrew

November 20, 1909

Andrew ran.

Jack was shouting at him, telling him to save his energy, but he didn't listen.

He ran because he couldn't stop himself. Even though his snowshoes were too loose and they pulled on his feet, even though his ankles ached and the wind felt like sandpaper against his skin — none of that mattered. He had plenty of energy. Here he would always have energy.

He ran because it was glorious, because the sky was so clear he thought he could see straight through to heaven. He loved the sound of the dry snow crunching beneath him and the hoarse chuffing of his own breath. In the distance, somewhere over the horizon line, the Transantarctic Mountains loomed craggy and blindingly white. Beyond them would be the South Pole.

He would be the first; Jack had agreed to it. Andrew would be the first person in history to step on the South Pole, and there he would proudly plant the flag of the United States of America. In the year 2000, when the world was different, when people would be traveling in time and taming the Martian frontier, they would point to Andrew Douglas Winslow for inspiration. He reached the end of the earth, they'd say. He made it possible for us to dream.

The expedition had been gone a week now. Maybe more. Andrew had lost track of time. He hadn't thought about the *Mystery*, or Colin, or home. Out here, your mind was always full. Out here, the basics were everything — breathing, seeing, running, eating.

Back home, he had read much about Antarctic weather. He knew that snow rarely fell here, that you worried more about the *blowing* ice and snow. But nothing had prepared him for the first blizzard — not the writings of Scott and London, not even the memory of the cruel ocean wind across the *Mystery*'s decks. On their second day out, the sun had abruptly vanished and the wind came in like fists. It threw the men back on their heels, causing the dogs to tumble and tangle in their traces. Like a comet's tail it spat ice and rocks, and Andrew had struggled to cover his face even as he felt his arms straining to stay in their sockets. In that moment his body became a machine, his mind an engine, useful only in their ability to propel him forward.

The storm had lasted all day, but the worst part came afterward, when the wind had died down. As the others set up camp in the lee of a rock formation, Andrew stood, numb and unable to move. This, he realized, was not an experience meant for humans. It was warfare against nature and destiny. A pack of fools tilting at an unvanquishable foe.

Andrew had awakened the next morning with tears frozen to his cheeks.

The sky was a brilliant blue. He stood and walked away from the camp, to where he could see the snow stretching in all directions, curving over the horizon line north, south, east, and west — or was it just north, north, north, and north? — and he smiled.

The bottom of the earth was, by the curious

laws of physics, also the top of the world. He knew that he had made it through the worst, alive — and if he could do that, he could make it all the way.

The team fixed a breakfast of pemmican, coffee, and hardtack and broke camp early. They mushed all day, breaking once for lunch. The second blizzard hit that night, fierce and punishing. But this time Andrew helped find shelter in a small ice cave. He loaded in the supplies, assisted in pounding the canvas over the opening, and helped light a fire.

For the next five days, the temperature had remained above zero — warm for Antarctica. They traveled twenty miles a day, easily.

And now Andrew wanted to see it all. Every inch.

As he ran, Socrates kept pace. Socrates was a renegade. An individual. He was different from the other dogs. Like Buck in *The Call of the Wild*, he couldn't be harnessed, couldn't stay in line.

Socrates ran because he needed to. He ran with Andrew.

"Where are we going next, Soc?" Andrew shouted, but the words seemed to freeze in midair and drop to the earth.

They were circling a steep ridge of snow, and Socrates pulled ahead in great leaping bounds.

He disappeared around the bend and suddenly started barking.

"What is it, boy?" Andrew called out.

He turned the corner and stopped in his tracks.

It was a field of ice baubles — small, mushroomlike, thousands of them packed together tightly, pulsing in the light, as far as he could see. They stood dense and orderly, as if they'd been planted.

The three sledges pulled up alongside Andrew. The dogs were jumping, howling at the sight.

Dr. Shreve, the geologist, ran toward the field, breaking off some of the specimens. Ruskey begged him to go away so he could set up a photo. Socrates, having pounced on an ice flower only to see it break into a knife-edged shape, now scampered back toward the sledges.

"Ice flowers!" Shreve called out. "Scott told about these."

"Ti oraia," Kosta murmured.

"It *is* beautiful, Kosta," Jack agreed. "Let's break, fellows. We'll camp behind the mound and have supper."

Jack retreated behind the hill. Kosta, Lombardo, and Dr. Riesman brought up the sledges behind him. As Andrew helped the other sailors set up tents, Riesman and Kosta fed the dogs.

O'Malley broke out the big stove and one Primus, fired them up, and reached into the food supplies. "Steaks are going fast," he said. "If you guys don't curb your appetites, we're in trouble."

"The place is crawling with seals," Cranston said.

Ruppenthal made a face. "Ugh."

"It's a delicacy in Kosta's country," Lombardo remarked.

"*Ti?*" Kosta asked.

"The food is supposed to last to the South Pole and part of the way back," Jack said. "As we get closer to the sea we hunt seals and penguins."

Andrew felt nauseated. "How far are we?" he asked.

"A long way, I'm afraid," Jack replied. "Six hundred miles or so — maybe seven more weeks. We've come about two hundred already. In two hundred fifty more, we'll be crossing the Transantarctics. That'll be the toughest part. Shackleton found a good pass, cut between the mountains by a glacier. We'll find one, too."

Dr. Shreve was unloading his supplies now,

packing ice-flower specimens into a box. But his eyes were fixed on the horizon. "What on earth is that?"

Andrew looked but saw only a small, clifflike ridge in the distance, off to the left.

"A hot cocoa factory, I hope," Lombardo said.

"Look at that outcropping," Shreve replied. "Exposed rock — schist, I think. This could be an extraordinary clue to the origins of this place."

"I suppose we could detour that way tomorrow —" Jack said.

"I'll go now. It may be nothing. Why waste everyone's time? I'll just need one sled, four dogs — Dimitriou, Taso, Kukla, Skylaki. No supplies. I'll cover the ground in no time. While I'm there, I can scout for a suitable path."

"David, you've lost your mind," Siegal said.

"I can't let you travel alone," Jack said. "You know that."

"The visibility is clear. I won't be traveling in darkness. It doesn't look far. There is no risk."

"Distances are deceiving here," Ruppenthal remarked.

Shreve was taking everything off the sledge, unhooking traces. "I know what I'm doing. I'll be back in a couple of hours. The dogs'll have time for a good night's sleep when I return."

"Let Kosta go with you," Jack said.

"Fine."

But Shreve was fast. He was on the sledge, mushing those dogs.

"Feeghe mazitou!" Jack called out.

Kosta looked startled. He ran off, calling to the dogs, *"Ella tho, paithakia mou!"*

"How do you know Greek?" Andrew asked.

Jack smiled. "I listen. I ask questions."

Shreve was long gone by the time Kosta was ready. O'Malley handed him a juicy cooked steak, which Kosta gnawed on as he rode off.

Andrew dug into his, using a fork and knife. The meat had to be eaten fast. It was cold by about the third bite.

The men crowded around the stoves, sitting on the remaining sledge and on the supply boxes. The wind had begun to pick up, and Andrew huddled tight, pulling on his gloves.

The sun had dropped behind the hill, on its way toward the horizon. Just before midnight it would set for a few minutes, then begin again its slow circle around the sky.

The men traded stories and jokes, until Lombardo challenged each man to reveal his darkest secret. "Me?" he began. "I once courted a young lady from Scranton by mail. She wanted my picture, but I thought my mug would scare her. So my brother, the theater agent? He lets me take a picture from his office one day — some actor, handsome guy, I don't know him from beans — and I send it."

"What'd she do when she saw your ugly face?" Siegal asked.

"She didn't. It turns out this guy's in all the magazines. Shaving cream ads. Toothpaste ads. Her old man takes one look at the picture, recognizes him, and says, I don't want you stepping out with no *model*. Which is why I am still a single man."

The men hooted with sympathy — or derision, it was hard to tell which.

The rest followed clockwise, one by one. Jack was second to last, Andrew last.

There were tales of sleepwalking and shoplifting, family tragedies and lost loves. But Andrew had a hard time concentrating. His eyes were on his stepfather.

They hadn't talked about Mother's death — not directly. He and Jack were birds of a feather. When the chips were down, you moved on. You ignored the things that couldn't be changed, the questions that nagged. Like why a meeting with Horace Putney was more important than a dying wife. Why a death couldn't even slow plans for an expedition, not even for a day.

Second-guessing corroded you. Made you bitter, like Colin. So you put it away in a corner of your brain until it hardened like a scab.

And you hoped no one asked you about it.

Andrew felt his stomach rumble. The day — June 10, almost a half year ago — was rushing back to him. Mother had called Jack's name. Her last moment was spent finding out that he wasn't there. He hadn't shown up to say good-bye.

Why? Why did he do it?

Don't, Andrew told himself. *Don't think.*

It was Jack's turn now. He said nothing for a long moment, until Ruppenthal bellowed out, "Louder and funnier!"

Jack smiled and shook his head. "Gentlemen, I must confess — I have nothing to say. I keep no secrets. I make my mistakes in the open."

The men broke into groans and catcalls.

In the open. That was how he saw it. He'd made his mistake in the open, and he didn't feel ashamed.

Or he felt he hadn't made a mistake at all.

Or he was lying.

Which?

Andrew would never find out. He didn't want to know.

It was in the past.

It would stay that way.

Now the men were looking at him.

"You can do better than that, can't you, sonny?" Lombardo asked.

The wind had picked up quite sharply, and snow fell in thick clumps. Andrew shivered and drew his knees up to his chest.

"Like father like son," he said softly.

15

Philip

November 20, 1909

"What do you mean, *you won't hunt*?"

Captain Barth's veins were jutting from his neck. Surely the fellow had medication for this ill humor. He wouldn't live long at this rate.

"I haven't been trained," Philip replied. "I'm afraid I wouldn't be of much use."

Some of the men in the cabin groaned. That was fine. This was all just fine.

"Captain," Hayes said. "I'll go in his place."

But Barth was intent on Philip. "You take a club. You walk up to the seal. You bring the club down on its head. Understand?"

Philip swallowed hard. The plan was working.

Barth looked sadistic, unrelenting. "It's like . . . cricket, then? Only for a ball you use the head of a smiling defenseless creature."

"Exactly!"

"Oh, I think I am going to be ill."

"Leave the boy alone," Brillman called out.

"Ah, Mr. Brillman," Captain Barth said. "Have you been appointed captain since we last spoke?"

"No, sir," Brillman murmured.

"I thought not. Well, you and Mr. Hayes may both go on the hunting party, since you seem so eager. And you will take young Master Westfall with you. To your posts, men!"

"Aye, aye, sir," the men called out.

As Barth climbed abovedecks, Philip leaned over to Brillman and Hayes. "I — I don't mean to be so helpless. It's just that — well —"

Brillman nodded. "You didn't develop a taste for hunting. My brother's like that. Doesn't mind trapping but can't bring himself to shoot. Too personal."

"Yes, that's it!" Philip said. "Captain Barth doesn't understand —"

"Barth is a pig," Hayes said. "He'd better watch who he gives a club to. I'm liable to bring it down over his fat head."

Hayes and Brillman.

Here were two. Two Highly Possibles.

Philip tried to control his glee. He shot a glance at Nigel.

Nigel winked.

16

Andrew

November 20, 1909

Five hours later, Kosta and Dr. Shreve hadn't returned.

The men had turned in. By 8:00 they'd been well fed and exhausted. Now it was after 10:30. The snow had turned to a blizzard, and Andrew was already deep into the first shift of the night watch.

The men had driven three posts into the snow and tied up the dogs, some of whom had dug themselves deep holes, curling up inside for warmth and shelter. The others, however, including Socrates, paced restlessly.

Andrew stayed inside his sleeping bag until he

couldn't hold off his curiosity. Throwing on his sweater and overcoat, he stepped outside.

The snow seemed to come at him from all directions. It made its way into his hood, his pockets, his boots as he edged away from the tents.

Just beyond the shelter of the hill, the wind hit.

It was like a solid thing. It knocked him off his feet and he dived to the ground. It flung snow at him like the edges of a thousand knives, shearing his skin and his tongue, taking away his ability to breathe.

Opening his eyes into this was impossible. He struggled upward, drawing his hood around his face, and stumbled back toward the tent.

"Stay put, there's nothing you can do to bring them back!" It was Jack, waiting by the flap, shouting to be heard over the wind. "Shreve is a smart man. More experienced than any of us. He's probably holed up somewhere, waiting for this to pass."

"What about Kosta?" Andrew asked.

"With any luck, they're together—" He stopped, cocking his head.

Andrew listened. Through the screech of the wind, he heard a sound. Percussive. Coming nearer.

Jack ran toward the open area beyond the hill, clinging to his wool watchcap.

The dogs leaped out of the wall of snow. They tackled Jack to the ground, yapping and licking his face.

Kosta was slumped over the sledge.

Andrew ran to help. He tried to lift Kosta, but he was deadweight. His skin was bone cold, his face blue.

Jack scrambled to his feet. He and Andrew grabbed the dogs' traces, but pulling them toward the tents was almost impossible. They were all worked up, jumping, trying to wrench away.

Siegal, Lombardo, and Cranston were awake, pulling on their parkas and rushing over to help. They lifted Kosta off the sled and dragged him into a tent.

Soon Ruppenthal and Petard were up, too. They helped Andrew and Jack pull the dogs.

"Where do they want to go?" Ruppenthal shouted.

"Back into the storm!" Jack replied.

"Why?" Petard asked.

"Ask *them*!"

"Come on, Plutarchos . . . shhh, shhh," Andrew said. "Taki, calm down."

Gradually they worked their way to the posts, tied the dogs, and ran back to the tent where Kosta had been taken.

Andrew had to elbow his way through the men who'd crammed inside. His hands were numb, and he removed his gloves to blow into his cupped palms. Everyone was awake now, kneeling around Kosta, who lay in the center in a sleeping bag covered with blankets. Dr. Riesman was examining him with a stethoscope.

"That's it, Siegal, massage his fingers, but gently," Dr. Riesman said. "Don't warm them too fast. The fingertips may be frostbitten a bit, but the damage isn't bad."

"He's going to be okay?" Jack asked.

Dr. Riesman nodded admiringly. "He's tough. Considering the amount of exposure, I'm amazed at his resiliency." He passed some smelling salts across Kosta's nose. "Kosta, can you hear me?"

Kosta's eyes fluttered. "*Poo . . . eemai?*"

The men burst into cheers.

"Yeeee-hah!" Andrew shouted. "He made it!"

"*Olla eenai entaksi,*" Jack said. "You're all right."

Kosta looked dazed and agitated. He peered around the tent. "Sreve? *Poo eenai* Sreve?"

"Shreve?" Jack said. "Do you know where he is?"

Kosta tried to rise to his feet, but Dr. Riesman held him down. "*Then vlepo!*"

"What's he saying?" Lombardo asked.

"He didn't see Shreve," Jack explained. "He wants to go back and find him."

He pushed his way toward the tent flap, pulling on his gloves.

"Where are you going?" Dr. Riesman asked.

"*I'll* find him," Jack replied.

"I'll go with you," Petard volunteered.

"No!" Siegal shouted. "We can't afford to lose you, too."

"We haven't lost *Shreve* yet," Jack said. "If he's snowbound, if he's in the same condition as Kosta, we can save him."

But before the men could move, a dog bounded through the flap. It was matted with snow, yowling terribly, and squirming away from the hands that reached for it, until it finally leaped onto Kosta.

It was Dimitriou. From Shreve's sledge.

He was alone.

And his traces were in shreds.

17

Colin

November 21, 1909

Andrew was there, right in front of him. He was riding away on a sledge but not facing forward, no, he was looking over his shoulder, staring at Colin, wanting to say something but all tongue-tied — and he couldn't see the iceberg that rose up before him, bursting from the earth like a monster god, the god of the Southern Frontier, flecked with black and red and brown, the bodies of its sacrifices, dinosaurs and seals and penguins and humans. It had a mouth, cavernous and black, that opened wide for Andrew with slavering greed — *Andrew, turn around, turn around, you fool* — Colin tried to shout the words but his mouth was paralyzed. He tried to point but his arms were dead. All of which made Andrew even more concerned; he was calling out to Colin now — *Colin, what's wrong with you? WHAT'S WRONG WITH YOU?* — but that wasn't the point, the sky was turning dark, the snow falling red, red as blood, red as death, and Andrew wasn't seeing it — *Why wasn't he seeing it?*

"Andrew!"

Colin sat up, banging his head on the wooden panels above.

"Will you shut your trap and go to sleep!" Bailey called out.

Wood. Wood and horsehair and the smell of wet wool and Bailey's voice.

He was on the ship. Safe and warm. There was no monster.

No Andrew.

"Sorry," Colin said.

It was so real. Like his dream about Mother seven years ago. And Stepmother, last June.

He had the power to see things no one else could. Mother had always told him that.

But this was just a nightmare.

There were no ice monsters. The snow didn't fall like blood.

Andrew was okay.

That's all. Just a nightmare.

Colin sank back into his bed.

But his eyes stayed open the rest of the night.

18

Jack

November 21, 1909

"That's it, Dimitriou! Good boy!"

The dog was way ahead, running alone, throwing up clouds of snow. Shreve's tracks were long gone, covered by the blizzard. But somehow the dog knew.

The two sledges moved slowly, loaded up with three sledges' worth of equipment. There was room for only one driver on each, and the men took turns while the others walked alongside. Jack was driving one, Petard the other.

They'd gone at least four miles. Shreve had covered a lot of ground, but the storm had come up too soon and he hadn't had time to return.

It was crazy to let him go, Jack thought, to let him just take off without waiting for Kosta. Shreve was a good man and an extraordinary scientist. But he was impulsive. Excitable.

Jack squinted against the morning sunlight. Never again. He would never let any of them out of his sight. They traveled together or not at all. A life was fragile here. The place could hypnotize you, then crush you in the snap of a finger.

Dimitriou had been taking a straight path. Dead ahead was the outcropping of rock that Shreve had wanted to see. But now the dog was angling to the right in a wide arc.

The sledges adjusted. But soon Dimitriou was tracing a path to the left. Then suddenly right again. Then backward, crossing over his own path.

"Heyyy-o!" Jack halted the sledges.

They waited and watched.

"Where's he going?" Petard asked.

"This must have been where Shreve hit the storm," Jack replied. "He lost his bearings, started backtracking."

Quickly Jack and Petard dismounted the sledges. Lombardo took over one, Oppenheim the other.

Dimitriou began barking loudly again, heading obliquely to the right. This time he was continuing.

"Move 'em out!" Jack shouted.

He trudged along behind Lombardo's sledge. Out of the corner of his eye, he took a head count. Thirteen, including himself. All present.

Andrew was with Oppenheim. In front of the pack. Running instead of walking. He was trying too hard. The boy was all heart. But he was a kid. At this rate, he was going to wear himself out.

"Conserve your energy, son!" Jack called out.

The ground was changing now, the powder giving way to long, wavelike ridges of ice and snow. The sledges jolted violently, slipping into the tracks between the ridges. Andrew took a spill, then Ruppenthal and O'Malley.

Sastrugi. Jack had read about these. The wind created them — a wind strong enough to shape solid ice.

Just beyond the sastrugi was a huge pressure ridge. Dimitriou stood beside it, yapping loudly and wagging his tail.

"'Attaboy!" Jack called out.

The two sledges pulled up beside the dog and halted. Lombardo and Oppenheim quickly climbed off and Jack ran up alongside them.

His heart stopped.

Hidden behind the ridge was a gash in the

earth. It began at their feet and widened to about twenty yards.

Dimitriou was whimpering now, walking in circles.

Jack looked down into the blackness but saw nothing.

One by one, the men took off their hats and lowered their heads.

"Lord, into Thy hands we commend the spirit of our brother David Shreve, a man of great intellect and physical courage."

Petard made the sign of the cross, completing his brief eulogy. Slowly the team began to file away from the crevasse.

Jack watched his men as they adjusted the sledges, hooking up Dimitriou to a new harness. Kosta was fighting back tears, muttering in Greek. Blaming himself, no doubt. Dr. Riesman was ashen and silent. He and Shreve had been friends since college.

Soon only Andrew remained by Jack's side.

"Son, I'm sorry —" Jack said.

"He was with us just a few hours ago," Andrew replied softly.

"The suddenness is a shock."

Andrew nodded and walked back toward the sledges.

Jack felt tongue-tied and feeble. This wasn't supposed to happen. He had vowed not to lose any men. Not one. Now, Shreve was dead.

He wanted to say something to Andrew. To the men. Something to lift them up, to take away the sting. That Shreve loved nature with such passion that it consumed him. That he died outdoors, exploring, the way he would have preferred it. But the words seemed hollow and cold. And they didn't tell the whole story.

He went because I let him go, Jack thought. *Because I didn't have the strength to say no.*

Jack tried to shake off the feeling. Guilt had no place in a trip like this.

Guilt was the enemy.

Siegal quickly took readings with his compass and sextant. He set them back on course, south by southeast. When Dimitriou was finally harnessed, they started again.

Thirty-two dogs were barely enough to pull the loads on the two sledges. The sky had filled with snow again, and the transantarctic winds roared from the south directly into their faces. Jack's Burberry parka couldn't keep out the cold. An icy rim had formed on the inside of his hood. Soon, if he didn't do something, it would close up solid, a mask of his own frozen breath. He'd be warmer inside it, perhaps, but he wouldn't be able to see. Or breathe.

Maybe that was just as well.

By the dimmed light of evening they approached a broad plain, scarred with crevasses. Ruskey reached for his camera. "There must be six of 'em. It's a polar canyon."

Siegal slowed his dogs. "Pop," he said, "if we get stuck in that place when the sun sinks, we can end up like Shreve."

"Then we'll have to go around it, won't we, Mr. Siegal?" Jack snapped.

"Aye, aye, sir."

Slowly they made their way across the plain. The wind pushed harder with each step.

Jack wrapped his scarf around his face, leaving only his eyes to the cold.

19

Philip

December 11, 1909

Smack. Tinkle.

Smack. Tinkle.

Smack. Tinkle.

This wasn't so bad, breaking the ice off the rigging. It had a kind of rhythm, a music to it. The other men had done the hard part — cleaned off the top. Philip merely needed to handle the bottommost . . . rigs. Or whatever you called these poles and ropes.

It was a shame, though, when you thought about it. Everything had looked so pretty covered with ice.

No, not ice. *Rime*. Rime was a marvelous thing.

It grew like moss — but it was water vapor, freezing on contact with a solid object. It built itself up, one particle on another, *into* the wind, exactly the opposite of what you'd expect.

Ice was what surrounded the *Mystery*. Pancake ice, to be exact, the flat, soft, snow-covered kind. It seemed perfectly harmless, yet Captain Barth was convinced they needed to move to safer water.

"Wake up, Westfall, before we hoist you with the sails!" Captain Barth called out.

"Aye, aye, O Mighty Captain."

Oops. Naughty.

Ah, well. Philip was no longer scared of Barth.

Much had happened in the month since the polar boys had left. Nigel had foreseen correctly, to Philip's great astonishment. Hayes and Brillman were easy recruits to the mutiny plan — and they, in turn, had convinced Bailey and Stimson.

Stimson, especially, was a relief. It would be murder to have to banish the cook to the brig. Nigel would no doubt insist on preparing the meals. Which in itself might cause a countermutiny.

They were a merry band of six now. They would need a few more. But there was still time. Plenty of time.

Across the deck a block of ice moved slowly,

carried atop a stout body. Flummerfelt, the motor expert. The thick-necked master of all things mechanical.

Barth had been hard on him over the months. Given him some of the worst jobs, such as carrying the ice to the mess for water. Flummerfelt should have been a Likely. But he was a loyal, unquestioning sort.

A Possible. Requiring special handling.

Philip quickly pounded his hammer against the rime until it was all gone.

As he jumped off and ran to the hatch, the crew began raising the sails.

"Oh, Mr. Flummerfelt!" Philip called as he descended. "Would you happen to have a copy of the nautical tables in your pocket?"

Flummerfelt turned. "Nautical tables?"

"Oh, I'm sorry, didn't mean to interrupt. I see Captain Barth has you on ice duty again. What have you done this time?"

Flummerfelt edged toward the galley and set the ice on the stove. "What do you mean?"

"Well, you must have done something to deserve this punishment. Captain Barth usually reserves the menial jobs for people he really hates, such as Nigel and myself. So I assumed you, who work so hard at the engine all day, would be exempt from such tasks unless you did something dreadful."

"I didn't do nothing dreadful," Flummerfelt said. "He just told me to do it."

"Yes, well, he does have his favorites. And his goats. Doesn't he?"

"Goats?"

"The ones he picks on. The ones he places himself above, by reason of education or breeding or whatnot. Some are easier targets than others, I suppose — in his mind."

"He ain't no better than me."

"Jolly good. That's what I say! Now quick, report back to him before he starts insulting you!"

Flummerfelt stalked away, red-faced.

Now Stimson was emerging from the hold, dragging up a frozen seal carcass.

What luck. What extraordinary luck.

"Ah, preparing the menu?" Philip asked.

"Nope," Stimson replied. "Cutting the blubber from Tubby over here."

"*You* do that? I thought your second cook was in charge of all the dirty work."

"O'Malley? He's with Pop. I'm alone now."

"And no one has been assigned to help you?"

"Ask the captain," Stimson said. "And step

aside in case he bites off your head, like he did mine."

Philip shook his head gravely. "Mm. How many years did you spend in culinary school?"

"Two. French cuisine was my specialty. Imagine that — and here I am, skinning animals and cooking blubber till I can't get it out of my skin."

"Well, I'm sure if Captain Barth weren't in charge, things would be different, wouldn't they?"

"I'll say!" Stimson laughed. "Hey, be careful what you wish for!"

"Oh, you bet I will," Philip said.

Very careful indeed.

That evening Philip and Nigel had floor duty in the afterhold. A useless task, with Stimson cooking seal. The air was rank with vaporized blubber, which settled like glue in the hair and the skin. No sooner had they cleaned a section of floor than it was slippery with grease.

"I fought you boiled that stuff outside," Nigel said.

"I do," Stimson replied. "This is the lean part."

"Well, I must say, you're truly a miracle worker. You're the only man wha' can make a tasty meal out of that slime, and my 'at is off to yer!"

Stimson smiled. "I do my best."

Philip elbowed Nigel in the ribs. "You're laying it on a little thick, aren't you?" he whispered.

"Wha' are you talkin' about? We've almost got 'im on our side. Won't 'urt to butter 'im up a bit."

Philip turned back to work, but he suddenly felt dizzy. His brush seemed to be slipping, not going where his hand put it. "Nigel . . . ?"

No, it wasn't him. He was fine. It was the ship. The *Mystery* was shuddering, rocking upward toward the port bow.

A saucepan clattered to the floor, spilling a gooey brown sauce.

Lovely, Philip thought. He'd need a chisel to clean that.

"All hands on deck!" shouted Mansfield into the hatch. "We're iced in!"

Philip's heart raced. He glanced at Nigel, who gave him a brief nod.

It was too good to be true. The Plan had been ready to execute for some time. All they needed was a way to get all of the men in one place, on the ice.

The way had been handed to them.

Nigel and Philip raced for the hatch.

"Blasted Barf," Nigel cried out, "runnin' us into pack ice again."

"He's using our ship as a battering ram," Philip said.

"The fool will sink us in no time," Stimson grumbled.

Good. Correct response.

On deck, the sailors were scrambling onto the kennels, then climbing over the gunwales. Mansfield threw picks, axes, and saws to the ice.

"If you get cold feet, I'll kill you," Nigel whispered.

"Poor choice of words," Philip replied.

Nigel quickly climbed over. Philip waited until Captain Barth was looking his way. Then he hoisted himself, as awkwardly as he could, onto the kennel.

"What're you doing?" Barth called out.

"Helping out the *Mystery*, sir!" Philip said crisply.

"Not after your performance last time. The men don't need entertainment. Get below and swab the decks."

Yes. Perfect.

Out of the corner of his eye, Philip spotted Bailey and the meteorologist, Talmadge.

Louder.

"But I want to help!" Philip protested. "It's my duty."

"It's your duty to obey orders!" Barth snapped.

"Captain, let the boy help out," Talmadge interrupted. "We need all the manpower we have."

"Whatever he has, it isn't *man*power," Barth said, turning away.

Philip drew his lips down and hung his head.

"Don't worry, kid," Talmadge said. "It ain't you. The man wouldn't know about leadership quality if it jumped up and bit him on the nose."

Philip nodded. He watched the two men climb over the gunwale.

Below, Nigel was waiting with Hayes and Brillman.

The three men took Talmadge and Bailey aside, away from the gas lamps and into the shadows.

Eight men . . . if this worked.

Philip smiled. It wouldn't be long now.

20

Andrew

December 11, 1909

"Jack!"

Calling was useless. Andrew was eating snow. Drowning in snow. The snow had become the atmosphere itself, the ground indistinguishable from the air. It was a continent exploding, rising up, falling back, swallowing him whole. Sucking out his energy and his will.

The ring of ice inside his hood wasn't any protection at all. It left a hole in the center where the snow blew in, hard and grainy, like sand. It packed up in the space between his face and the ice, and it stayed there.

His lips were cracked, the blood freezing the moment it oozed out. His cheeks were scraped dry by the wind and snow.

He was alone. The sledges were gone. He'd been holding a tie line with the others, but he was tired and numb, and the line was covered with ice and the ground was ice and he couldn't hold on, so he fell and let go, and suddenly everything had vanished.

Now he couldn't see and couldn't hear through the storm.

And soon he couldn't walk, so he fell to his knees.

He put his head down to the wind. He would stop. He had to stop. Just for a minute.

He listened to his own breath. It sounded far away, like someone else's, someone in the next room.

He could stay here. Just temporarily. Soon it would be over. Soon the storm ended. It always did. He could stay here and be warmer and wait.

Holes.

That was how the dogs slept — in holes. The snow insulated them, trapped their body warmth. He would need a hole.

So he began digging. His gloves were frozen solid, natural shovels. In the soft snow he was able to chop out a shelter in no time.

He crawled into it. He turned on his side and felt his body sink in, curled up tight.

His face was out of the line of fire. The snow strafed him from above, pelting his coat, but his face was protected.

Here it was quiet.

He could stay until it was over. He could close his eyes and let them relax.

That was it. Just rest — not sleep. Never sleep. Sleep was the first sign of death.

Rest and think of home, think of the fireplace and the frost on the windows and the snow-dusted cobblestones of Bond Street, and Jack and Colin, and Mother, too — she's saying, Rest. Rest, darling. It's all right. You'll be all right. I'll see you soon.

And then he was moving. Sliding forward. Choking. He could feel the snow on his face again, sharp and hot — something was pulling him by the neck, taking him from the hole, which made no sense because he was safe here, this is what the dogs did, and the dogs *knew*. . . .

He dug his hands and his legs into the snow but he couldn't feel them, he couldn't feel anything, he was all mind and no body, and beside him right in his ear was a chuffing sound, a heavy breathing, and he forced his eyes open to see a thick mat of ice-covered fur.

"Socrates?"

The dog let go of Andrew's collar and barked, a scolding, get-up-and-come-with-me bark, and Andrew tried to propel himself but only succeeded in falling facedown in the snow.

"Socrates . . . just *go* . . . get help!"

But Socrates tried again, clamping down on the jacket, pulling from his haunches, until Andrew found the strength to twist himself around and kneel into the snow.

He could feel his legs now. The blood was flowing.

Socrates released his jaw. He rose up, placing his forepaws on Andrew's shoulders, breathing heavily, trying to lick him.

It was warm, so warm. It felt good on his skin, on his eyes. "My hands, Soc, please!"

He turned his back to the wind and pulled off his gloves. His hands were blue-white, the skin like parchment.

Socrates began licking them, but Andrew felt nothing.

The pain started in his palms, an itch that quickly became sharp and agonizing. The dog's tongue felt like sandpaper, and Andrew pulled his hands back.

And then, without warning, Socrates was gone. His bark faded into the roar of the blizzard.

Andrew blew into his hands. He flexed them and blew on them until the pain was excruciating, but he knew that was good, that the first sign of frostbite was when you felt absolutely nothing.

A few moments later he heard voices. Shouts.

He tried to yell but his vocal cords were shot. He staggered to his feet, bracing himself against the snow, the pain.

A moment later Socrates leaped out of the whiteness, barking at the top of his lungs — and this time he was not alone. Five dogs emerged from the snow behind him, pulling a sledge. They were haggard and silent, panting heavily, their brows caked with snow and ice.

Andrew heard Jack's voice before he could make out the face.

"Andrew!"

"*Kalò to Theòs!*" Kosta was with him.

Jack jumped off the sledge and wrapped his arms around Andrew's shoulder. "Can you walk?"

"I think so. A little."

As Jack and Kosta helped Andrew to the sledge, the dogs hardly gave a glance. They were shivering. Even padded by snow they looked thin. They'd been fine for the first three weeks of the journey, but many had come down with dysentery. Taki, Yanni, and Loukoumada had already been buried. The five who were here surely hadn't needed this detour to rescue Andrew.

Jack sat Andrew in the sledge, facing away from the wind. He had two blankets, which he wrapped around Andrew, then dug out snow and ice from inside Andrew's hood.

Kosta handed Jack the reins. "You stay with boy. Kosta walk."

Jack mushed the dogs. Slowly the sledge began to move. Under the blankets, Andrew began feeling warmer. As the numbness left him, the pain in his hands began to spread until he was shaking uncontrollably.

"Andrew —?" Jack said.

Kosta peeled off his heavy parka and handed it to Jack. "Take — for boy!"

"Kosta, you need that!" Jack replied.

"Have other!" Kosta said, pointing to a thin jacket he was wearing. "Me run. Warm. *Zèsti.*"

Jack threw the coat around Andrew and held him tight with one arm as he guided the sledge.

Andrew's teeth were chattering and he barely heard the distant barking from the other sledge. It came into sight, hard against the side of a large pressure ridge.

"Bravo!"

Petard was leading a cheer. Andrew tried to acknowledge, but he could barely move.

Both sledges were moving now — uphill, the wind at their backs.

"Stop at the summit!" Jack commanded. "We'll find a path down the other side, away from the wind!"

The sledge gave an abrupt jerk. Jack yanked on the reins, halting the movement as Kosta sprinted to the front.

One of the dogs — Plutarchos — had fallen. Kosta scooped him up, tearing off his harness. "Go!"

Jack mushed the dogs again. The other men hadn't even stopped. They trudged ahead, leaning into the slope of the hill.

Kosta was falling back now, slowed by the weight of the dog.

"Slow down!" Andrew called to Jack. "We need to get —"

"Who-o-oa!" Jack shouted. He halted the dogs and jumped off the sledge.

But he wasn't heading toward Kosta.

Andrew glanced over his shoulder. The men were all gathering in a line at the top of the hill.

Kosta was out of sight now, lost in the snow. Andrew threw his legs over the side of the sledge. His body cried out in pain as he climbed out. Slowly he walked back along the sledge tracks, into the wind.

If he hadn't noticed a slight movement within the whiteness to his left, he would have missed Kosta.

Plutarchos shivered in Kosta's arms. They were both lying in the snow.

"Come on!" Andrew said, grabbing Kosta by his jacket.

"Me . . . not . . . walk. *To pothi mou!* Me foot."

"Give me the dog!"

Kneeling down, Andrew took Plutarchos in one arm. The dog was alarmingly light, thin and fragile from sickness. Then Andrew put his other arm around Kosta's shoulder.

Kosta leaned heavily on him. The pain was sudden and excruciating. Andrew cried out. "I — I can't —"

"*Ella!*" Kosta shouted. "Come!"

The tracks were still visible, but the snow was eating them up fast. Andrew willed his legs forward. He couldn't give up. With him, all three could make it. Without him . . .

Right. Left. Right.

"Andrew!"

It was Jack's voice.

Andrew and Kosta both yelled back, a desperate, wordless howl.

The men descended on them. Ruskey and Lombardo helped Kosta away, Rivera took Plutarchos, and Andrew felt Jack's firm grip around his shoulders.

They walked to the top of the slope and looked over.

The hill ended in a sharp drop-off, almost straight down. Andrew could see maybe 200 feet, but that was it. The snow obliterated sight of the bottom. "What do we do now?" he asked.

"Go back and circle around," Siegal suggested. "What else can we do?"

"In this wind — with the dogs sick?" Lombardo shook his head. "We'll never make it."

Andrew stared at the whirling snow. As it swept away from the ridge in great bursts, he caught momentary glimpses of the wall's lower part. It seemed to slope outward. "We could slide," he said.

Rivera laughed.

"Suicide," Oppenheim said.

Jack was squinting over the ledge. "It looks as if there's a valley down there. If we stay here, the cold'll kill us. If we make it to the bottom, we'll be on the lee side. We can take shelter there until the storm breaks."

The men turned in to one another, wary and beleaguered.

"Is that an order, Pop?" Ruppenthal asked.

"Sledges first," Jack said. "Then dogs. Then us."

The first sledge went without a fuss, shooting straight down the wall on its runners. The second hit a rock. It teetered to one side, then flipped into the air. "No!" wailed Oppenheim as the contents of the sledge — stoves, food, tent supplies — flew off.

As each item pitched downward, vanishing into the storm, Andrew's hope went with them. They couldn't make it without the supplies. Most of the food was on that sledge.

The other men had seen it. They knew the implications. But they were carrying on. He needed to carry on, too. Kosta was struggling with the frightened dogs, beckoning for Andrew's help.

Together they cajoled Socrates into going over first. Three others followed willingly. Seven were too weak to resist. The rest snarled and snapped. Kosta couldn't do much from a sitting position; his feet were useless. Finally the men had to gang up and send them over, one by one. Ruppenthal received an ugly gash on his arm for his efforts; Cranston struggled with a combative husky and ended up going over with it.

Jack was the next man to go. Kosta followed, bellowing with an ungodly shriek. The others followed, counting to 160 between trips to give the others a chance to clear.

Andrew was last.

He tried to see the others but couldn't.

His body seized up. He imagined sliding to the bottom, landing among a pile of corpses and supplies. This was insane. They didn't *know* what was down there.

But he knew what was up here.

He had no choice.

He pushed himself over, and suddenly he was in the air, not sliding but flying, borne on the snow and wind — until his rear end slammed onto the ice and he tumbled, out of control, trying to stay on his back for fear the ice would rip off his face.

He could see nothing but he felt the angle change, growing more horizontal, until he was sliding past shadows — and they were running after him.

Andrew came to a stop in a snowbank. He lay there, feeling his heart thrum, as the men ran toward him — Jack, Petard, Cranston, Rivera.

Jack lifted Andrew out of the snow. "Well?"

"Fun," Andrew said woozily. "Can we do that again sometime?"

"Central Park's more my speed." Jack hugged him tightly. "I'm afraid the weather's no better down here."

"Worse," Cranston shouted.

As they stepped out from the snowbank, the blizzard barraged them. Andrew tried to turn his face, but it didn't help. The wind seemed to be coming from all directions at once.

"We're getting close to the mountains!" Jack shouted. "They're causing this wind-tunnel effect. The wind races down the slopes and is blocked by this ridge — it has no place to go."

"We're finally near the Transantarctics?" Andrew asked.

"Don't get too excited," Jack replied. "It's another month to the Pole after we cross them."

"*If* we cross them," Rivera remarked.

"We're setting up camp, about fifty yards northeast," Jack said. "We've lost a lot of the food supply, but Petard thinks he knows where it is."

"I spotted something by the base of the ridge, to the east of the campsite," Petard explained. "Follow me."

Andrew stayed close to the four men as they trudged against the wind. Before long Andrew saw a dark shape in a distant, upward-sloping bank of snow. "There it is!" Andrew cried out.

"What?" Cranston asked.

"Something!"

Just ahead of them a low, hideous rumble began. It was soft at first, like the distant calving of an iceberg from a shelf into the sea. But there was no shelf here, no sea.

The men stopped.

Jack grabbed Andrew by the shoulders and turned him around. "Run — all of you!"

The earth was shaking now, the rumble now a crashing of rock and ice, growing louder. The ridge was giving way, breaking apart into an avalanche.

Andrew felt shards of ice pelting his back and

legs. He fell to the ground with a yell, and Jack yanked him to his feet. "*Fly!*"

His legs churned. He took in gulps of frozen air that seared his lungs.

But the noise stopped as suddenly as it had started. And by the time they'd reached camp, the only sound Andrew heard was the howling of wind.

The tents were flapping angrily, the men gathered in concern and terror by the openings. They raced toward Andrew and the others.

"You boys all right?" Ruskey called out.

"All present . . . and accounted for," Jack shouted, panting. "Wish I could say the same for the food."

In the silence, the men stared at a distant, growing shape. Through the white storm was a denser cloud, rising darkly — the fallen snow, tons of it, billowing like dust in a desert wind.

Had they remained a moment longer, Andrew knew they'd have been buried inside.

"We were lucky," Petard said.

Rivera's arms were tracing the sign of the cross. "*This* time."

As Andrew caught his breath, he saw O'Malley stoking his stove outside another tent. Ruppenthal intently held an ax over the flame. The blade was red hot.

Andrew staggered closer. “What are you doing?”

The two men looked at each other. Neither answered.

A scream from inside the tent made Andrew’s hair stand on end.

“O’Malley,” Andrew said tentatively, “how’s Kosta?”

“Dr. Riesman took a look at his feet,” O’Malley answered.

“Frostbite?”

“Worse. Gangrene.”

“Does that mean Kosta has to lose his —?”

O’Malley nodded grimly.

Andrew glanced at the ax. He felt sick.

21

Kosta

December 11, 1909

The cold was supposed to stop the pain.

It didn't.

It made everything worse. So much worse. The men were fading in and out and Kosta hoped they would just disappear, *poof*, and he would be free from the pain, free from the cold, free from this earth, free.

Riesman was a kind man, to be an animal doctor you had to be a kind man, so why did he do this? What kind of man used an ax on another man while he was awake? In Nísyros, in the tiniest back-road *chorià* of Greece, you didn't treat a goat like that.

Now he was useless. His feet were bloody stumps. At least with the toes he could force himself to walk. Without them, what? What was the point in taking away a man's toes and expecting him to go on? Did they plan to carry him on the sledges, like the *papou* in the old country, the lame grandfathers who had to be carted around in wheelbarrows until they died? Not here. This was not Greece. This was a hell from which there was no release. They were in danger. They didn't need Kosta.

He tried to tell them — *God have mercy, leave me, leave me to freeze, to go peacefully in the cold* — but the words wouldn't come, just the moaning and the pain, and he could see the blood in bright red clumps of ice on the ground.

Jack was talking. Holding Kosta's hands. "*Allos eenai entaksi.*" Everything is all right.

But it wasn't, it would never be, they were all doomed if they slowed down; they had to cut their losses and move on. Didn't he see that? Was this his idea of compassion, risking the lives of an entire group for one man?

The words flew around him in the tent, English words. The men were arguing. They never understood Kosta's Greek — only Jack did — so they assumed Kosta didn't understand them. But they were wrong, and they were stupid, because they were talking about him and he understood.

He's dying.

The dogs are dying.

We're dying.

Siegal, Rivera, Ruskey — they were afraid. They wanted to move on, save as many as they could.

We need him, Jack was saying. *He will heal. He will walk.*

Only Riesman was paying Kosta attention, trying to stop the bleeding, doing things that made Kosta shriek with pain — and when his leg jerked, the blood from his stumps flew into the men's faces and all over the dogs and the canvas.

"Stop it! Just stop it!" The boy, Andrew. So loud. He was never loud. "Listen to you all — 'Is he too heavy, is he going to eat all our food, will he slow us down' — he's not a *thing*. He's a man. The best one of us all. He's telling us to leave him. Would you do that? Would any of you offer to sacrifice yourselves?"

No.

No, he's a child. A dreamer. All he knows, everything in his head, comes from books. Heroes and villains, virtue and evil. He hasn't lived long enough to know destiny, to know that men controlled nothing, that all you could do was hear when God was calling and know that it was time to say yes.

"We're only as strong as our weakest member," Andrew went on. "Right? I mean, isn't that what separates us from the animals? Isn't that what makes us human? Were you relieved when Dr. Shreve died? No. So what happened since then? What changed you?"

They were all listening, silent. Taking the boy seriously.

"If we leave Kosta," the boy said, "we're saying a life doesn't matter. And if those are the rules now — well, who's safe? Any one of us can be deadweight. Any one of us can be left behind. If that's what we've become, what's the point of going to the South Pole?"

"It's going to be hard enough making it, even without the Greek," Rivera said.

"Maybe we should split," Ruppenthal suggested. "Some of us should wait here. The others go off to the Pole, with the dogs who aren't sick."

"Are you crazy, Rupp?" Siegal said. "No one can survive here, standing still. Besides, we'd never find each other again."

“So what do we do?” Cranston asked.

“Feégheteh,” Kosta said feebly. “You go.”

He forced his eyes open. The faces stared down at him, shadowed by the hoods.

“Yes, Kosta,” Jack said. “We go.”

Finally. A wise decision. The American was using his head.

Kosta let his body relax. Sleep quickly began to overtake him.

Peace.

Rest.

At last.

“Pop,” Petard said, “do you mean — we’re *all* —?”

“Yes. All of us,” Jack replied. “Kosta, too. We’re going back to the ship.”

Kosta was suddenly wide awake. “No!” he blurted out.

“Sir?” Ruskey said.

“We lost half our food over the side of that cliff,” Jack replied. “The seals and penguins don’t come this far inland — so once we run out, we starve. The dogs are sick and weak. We’ll be lucky if they last another month.”

“What do we tell them back at the ship?” Siegal asked. “They waited for us for no reason?”

Lombardo's face was red, contorted with anger. "We'll eat less and run faster. You're telling us to give up! We can't fail. Our mission was to find the South Pole."

"To find it *together*, Vincent — and return alive. You're not a failure if God and nature stop you — only if you resist them when it becomes impossible. You fail if you defeat yourself. Our team didn't do that. We knew how to prepare, we knew how hard to fight — and now we must know when to turn back. Frankly, I intend for this mission to be a success. Only now success means something different — it means a safe return to the *Mystery* for all of my men."

Oppenheim let out a soft, derisive snort. "Is that an order . . . *sir*?"

"Yes," Jack said. "Pack up now. We move when the storm breaks. Finding a way around that ridge will be hell."

Part Four

Retreat

22

Colin

December 31, 1909

"This is between me and you. I mean, all this stuff I just told you — anyone asks, I didn't say nothing, right?"

Flummerfelt was a monster. The strongest sailor on board by a long shot. He could lift a 100-pound box of tackle onto his shoulder like a sack of grain.

Above the neck, however, he was traveling short-sail.

Nigel and Philip must have had a grand time at his expense. Telling him they would organize a *mutiny*? Those two couldn't organize a tea party. This had to be some strange New Year's prank. Captain Barth had refused to allow a party, and the men were starved for entertainment.

Colin would have to set him right in a hurry. They were alone in the afterhold, but not for long. All hands were chopping ice. If Colin didn't return abovedecks with sledgehammers and harpoons — and Flummerfelt — Captain Barth would have their heads.

"Nigel is a stowaway," Colin said. "He has no legal rights on this ship. And he isn't much of a sailor. Now, how can someone like that lead a ship like the *Mystery*?"

"Same question as what I asked. But, see, that's why they need me. You, too. I seen you up there, an' you know your way around the deck. Captain Barth? He'll let us stay here until the ship is crushed. He's depressing the workingman, like Nigel says. Anyways, in the new order, I'll be first mate." Flummerfelt smiled proudly. "You'll be my second. They've stockpiled some weapons in the storeroom. Can you load a rifle?"

"Wait. Have you seen these weapons?"

"Sure. I helped load 'em. Some of these guys has never done that before, so that's why I'm asking. Anyways, Talmadge brought some guns onto the ice this morning. I was supposed to bring the rest. Now we can both do it."

Colin was stunned. This was no joke.

But it made no sense. Sure, the men had been grumbling about Barth for a while. But then they'd been grumbling about a lot of things — the ship, the weather, the lack of Christmas festivities, one another. They couldn't seriously intend to take the ship back and strand half the crew on the ice.

"And my father's party?" Colin asked. "We're just supposed to leave them?"

Flummerfelt's face dropped. "They say he ain't coming back, Colin."

"Who says that?"

"Nigel . . . Philip," Flummerfelt said hesitantly. "A few of the others, too — Bailey, Hayes, Brillman."

"So the idea is, cut our losses and save ourselves? Leave them for dead before we have any definite knowledge? This is Philip's thinking, isn't it?"

"Look, Colin, I never should have mentioned this to you," Flummerfelt murmured. "Don't tell nobody I said —"

"Are the men actually following *Philip*?"

"He's tougher than you think, Colin. All that

high-and-mighty talk? An act. Seems he's a dangerous outlaw —"

Colin burst out laughing. "And I'm the czar of Russia!"

"He's got newspaper clippings. Nigel showed me. Philip is wanted by the police — the *London* police. Look!" Flummerfelt stomped over to Philip's bunk, pulled open the curtain sheet, and reached into an unlocked chest underneath. "They're in here somewhere."

He riffled through a pile of papers and fished out a yellowed news clipping.

Colin took it and read:

Public-school vandals . . . weaponry was most likely toy guns . . . "a lark," Sergeant Hollings said. "These boys have had it handed to them for so long, they believe they deserve it" . . . "any theft of £10,000 from a London bank has to be taken seriously, and those young men treated as adult criminals and prosecuted to the full extent of the law" . . . A warrant has been issued for the arrest of . . . Philip Westfall . . . to be treated as armed and dangerous . . .

"It sounds like a prank," Colin said. "A stupid schoolboy prank that turned dangerous. Did you read this?"

"Well . . . yes. I mean, I know the gist of it . . ."

Flummerfelt looked at the article, his brow furrowed deeply. He pointed to the first paragraph. "Read this part — aloud, like. So I can recall it."

Colin cringed.

Of course. He should have known.

"These big words on top?" Colin said patiently. "They say, 'Boys Will Be Boys — Upper-Class Thieves Honing Their Skills on the Backs of the Working Class.'"

23

Jack

December 31, 1909

"It's his heart."

Dr. Riesman tried to save him and blew into his mouth.

Jack felt helpless. He stood there, crouched under the low ice ceiling of a cave in the middle of nowhere, with his stepson on one side and a makeshift hospital on the other, and he hadn't the slightest idea what to do.

In the list of all that could go wrong — accidents, frostbite, maritime collisions, rebellion, starvation, snow blindness — he had never thought to include heart problems.

One minute Lombardo was like everyone

else — frozen, weary, numb from a two-week retreat through a constant blizzard. They'd been moving slowly but steadily, each man catching sleep only when it was his turn at the sledge. When they'd stumbled on this bleak, tiny cave, Lombardo had staked out a corner and begun hacking the ice off his sleeping bag, which had frozen solid. Just like everyone else.

Then the convulsions started, and his face was blue.

Dr. Riesman instantly took over. And he was still at it, steady, emotionless, a real pro. One, two, three, blow.

The cave felt like a tomb. Two gas lanterns flickered over Dr. Riesman's shoulders, hung on pegs that had been driven into the ice walls.

The men were watching, but barely. They'd repelled sleep for days, and it wouldn't capitulate any longer.

One, two, three, blow.

Lombardo's body jerked. He coughed twice. Spittle oozed down the side of his mouth.

"Riesman . . ." Lombardo mumbled, his voice little more than a hoarse whisper.

"Yes, Lombardo," Dr. Riesman said.

"I — I didn't know you cared."

That idiot grin. That stupid sense of humor.

"He's back," Andrew murmured.

"Merry Christmas," Jack said.

"When was Christmas?" Rivera asked.

Dr. Riesman drew a blanket over Lombardo. "You rest."

"Are you going to have to shoot me, Doc?" Lombardo asked.

"Not today. Ask me again in the morning."

Lombardo's eyes shut. He was out.

Jack sat back against the cave wall. Around him, the men looked wind-burned and scruffy. In seven weeks, none of them had shaved or washed.

A pile of ice shards lay against the back wall, all of it hacked off the men's sleeping bags. A questionable achievement, since the bags had frozen through. Body warmth would only turn the remaining ice into wetness. Of course, that might not ever happen. The temperature in the cave was –15° F.

The men had barely reacted to Lombardo's plight. They were little more than nerve endings now. Reaction. Self-protection. Propulsion.

They needed rest. And they would have it, Jack decided. They would stay here for days if they had to. As long as it took for them to resemble humans again. They had made it this far — 450 miles out, maybe 350 back — they couldn't give in now, when they were so close.

"Will he —?" Jack asked.

Dr. Riesman nodded. "It was a mild attack. He'll be all right."

He quickly put away his stethoscope, gave Jack a cursory nod, and fell asleep on the snow-packed floor.

Oppenheim peered out of his sleeping bag. "Poor guy. Would have been luckier if he died now and got it over with."

"Look at it this way — he'll have plenty of good stories to tell when we get home," Jack offered.

"*If*, Pop," Oppenheim replied. "*If*."

Jack said nothing. Oppenheim's attitude had grown poisonous. He was pulling the men down with his nervous bleakness.

Pessimism was a sickness. If you fed it, it spread. Sometimes it was best to leave it alone. Let it wear itself out. Oppenheim's eyes were closing.

Jack felt the weight of Andrew's head on his shoulder. The boy had fallen asleep, too.

Jack was now the only one awake.

Gently he set Andrew down on the ground. He removed his parka and covered the boy with it.

Andrew was a good kid.

He hadn't lost his will, like some of the others. Maybe his youth made him more resilient. Maybe he realized that he was lucky to be here, that he'd have a chance to do it again someday.

Or maybe he was just putting on a good show.

Jack checked Lombardo's pulse. It was steady.

He peered outside the cave. The dogs were in their holes, still as the dead. He wondered how many would wake up.

Next to the dogs the supply tent was iced through and sagging.

At least the blizzard had let up. Now the weather was merely dismal. A run of dismal weather would be good luck.

Jack's eyelids felt like lead weights. His body shook, and he didn't bother trying to control it.

Andrew had been scheduled for the first night-watch shift, but Jack couldn't wake him. No one deserved to be awakened.

No harm in taking a shift or two himself. Eventually someone would wake up and relieve him.

Jack stood in the cave door. He considered taking his parka back from Andrew, but that wouldn't be fair. The boy was smaller; he needed it more.

Besides, the cold was good, Jack decided. It would keep him awake.

To keep his hands warm, he put them in his trouser pockets. And he felt a small, unfamiliar object there and pulled it out.

It was a flag. The cartographer — Walden — had given it to him in Argentina. Jack was supposed to have given him something in return — for good luck. But he hadn't. What did that mean? Was it bad luck not to return the gesture? Was that why the trip had failed?

Stop.

It was only a superstition. He had to block it out.

He began running in place to keep the circulation up.

Run, he told himself. Keep those eyes open. Try not to shake. Ignore the cold. Think straight, don't let yourself sleep, think about lists, about the ship, about debts, the Bond Street house mortgage, the dry goods shop around the corner, don't let yourself sleep, that idiot Horace Putney, Lowell the old college roommate who turned his back on financing the trip, the green grass of Harvard Yard and the excitement of sneaking into the boathouse — with Lowell, as a matter of fact — it was his fault, really, stealing the oar and sawing off the paddle, attaching wheels to the bottom so they could skate with it, oh was that fun, and if Lowell had been caught *he'd* have been expelled instead of me and I wouldn't have gone to the Yukon and married Raina and had Colin and none of this would have happened. . . .

In the distance Jack spotted an unusual, languid movement. A long, dark object was gliding toward him fast.

He recognized the shape, the rhythm, and he smiled.

It was a kayak. Raina's kayak. She was in it. Smiling. Surrounded by light. Light and warmth.

I've been expecting you, he said.

She stopped paddling but the kayak was still going . . . rising now . . . upward. . . . She called his name and told him to come. She had new places to show him.

Jack stepped forward, into the wind.

The snap of the cold made him gasp — and the image was gone.

Raina was gone.

Not Raina. A dream. A waking dream. A death dream.

The cold was taking him. He needed warmth. He needed dry clothes, a sleeping bag.

No. He couldn't take from the men. He could

hold out until after his shift. Let the men rest. That was the most important thing.

Two hours. That was all. He just had to keep his eyes open for two hours. Then he could switch. Then he'd be all right.

Maybe he didn't have to stand the whole time.

He squatted and felt his legs creak. They hurt, so he sat.

All he had to do was keep his eyes open. Stay awake.

It wasn't Raina. Not really.

She was gone.

Like Iphigenia.

And Shreve.

Their faces appeared before him now, all three of them, and he suddenly felt warm, head to toe, toasty and comfortable and surrounded by light and love. It thrilled him to know that they were so close, and he wanted to thank them, ask them how they'd been, but all they did was beckon. *Come. Come with us, Jack. Don't suffer.*

They were phantoms, this wasn't real. But the warmth was. He had stopped shaking and he felt no snow, no chunks of flying ice, no bitter cold. Lord knows he needed that, and so what harm would it be to stay this way a little longer, to give in for a moment.

It wouldn't hurt.

Jack let his eyes close.

And he gave in.

24

Colin

December 31, 1909

"I think I found it! The barrel's empty." Flummerfelt called out from the hold. "It says *G–U–N–P–O–W–*"

"Yes. That's it," Colin said. "Hurry up!"

Captain Barth's voice shouted from above deck: "What are you two waiting for, an engraved invitation?"

"Aye, aye, right away!" Colin replied.

"Done!" Flummerfelt said. He scrambled out of the hold with two rifles, a sledgehammer, and a harpoon.

Colin pulled open his bunk curtain sheet and

helped Flummerfelt hide the arms under the horsehair.

Grabbing the hammer and harpoon, they ran upstairs. Flummerfelt went over the gunwale first, carrying both implements in one hand.

Colin leaped atop the kennels. Below, the men hacked away at the ice that now encroached on the *Mystery* from all sides.

From behind the ship's stern, he heard Nigel's voice.

Nigel was supposed to be at the bow. All the men were.

Colin slipped back down onto the deck. Quietly he walked abaft and crouched low.

It wasn't just Nigel.

"By all means, let's be quick about this. No tedious speeches about the condition of the workingman." Philip's voice. Naturally.

Raising himself slowly, Colin peered over the ship. Nigel and Philip were digging a shallow trench directly beneath him.

Fifty feet away, Talmadge emerged from behind a pressure ridge. In his arms were three rifles and a pistol.

"Catch us a lot of seals wif that, won't we, mate?" Nigel said.

Talmadge dumped the guns in the trench, then clapped his hands like a seal and croaked quietly, *"Barth! Barth! Barth!"*

"Just get on with it!" Philip pleaded.

The three kicked snow over the weapons, enough to hide them from sight.

Just as Flummerfelt had said. They'd brought some of the weapons out earlier and hidden them from sight. Now they were stashing them closer to the ship for quick retrieval when the mutiny began.

"What about the rest?" Philip asked.

"Stumblefelt is bringin' 'em up," Nigel said. "If 'e can find 'em."

"Fine," Philip said. "Let's do this before Barth finds out and hangs us."

Colin sneaked back to the kennels. He climbed over the hull and onto the ice.

Talmadge, Bailey, Hayes, and Stimson were chopping ice at the prow, looking guilty as sin. Soon Philip and Nigel joined them, along with Flummerfelt.

"The picks are all in use, Winslow," Captain Barth said, approaching out of the darkness. "Take a chisel and use that sledgehammer, will you?"

"What's the plan, Captain?" Colin asked.

"I think we made a mistake anchoring here. My fault. For the last few days there's been a water sky to the northeast. Chances are, if we move there we'll be free of the ice — and in position to move farther away when the weather turns."

"Any good leads through the pack?"

"About a hundred yards away. If we break the ship loose, I think we can make it at full steam. It's really our only choice."

"Otherwise, the currents will pull us the other way, clockwise," Colin said.

"Exactly, sailor." Barth's lips curled up in what undoubtedly was a smile. "I'm glad someone besides Mansfield is using his head on this ship. Now get to work."

Colin set the wedge into the ice and began to smack it with the hammer.

Flummerfelt was glancing at him. Something was up.

Colin counted Nigel's gang. Six, including Flummerfelt.

Bailey was missing.

Now Stimson was stepping away, disappearing behind the prow. Talmadge, Hayes, Nigel, and Philip remained.

Their plan was starting. Colin hoped Flummerfelt had remembered what to do.

Stimson returned, agitated. He whispered something to Flummerfelt. With a questioning look, Flummerfelt pantomimed climbing a ladder.

He was sending Colin a signal. They had a ladder on the other side. They were going back up to the ship for the other weapons.

Stimson, Flummerfelt, and Nigel disappeared around the ship. Four gone now.

Thunk. Thunk. Thunk.

Colin broke off an enormous chunk of ice, opening a crack that spread down the hull, toward the prow.

The *Mystery* righted itself, sending a swell of water up through the ice. It was free.

One by one, the crew turned to Colin. Two or three started applauding. What had this boy eaten for breakfast? Windham asked. Let him pull the ship himself, Robert said.

But Colin kept his eye trained on the prow.

In the commotion the last two slipped away — Philip and Hayes.

Seven men were on Nigel's team altogether.

Barth, Mansfield, Dr. Montfort, Windham, Kennedy, and Colin were left. Only six.

Colin unbuttoned his parka. The temperature was barely above zero, but he was sweating. Any moment now . . .

"All right, drop the picks — everybody! Put your 'ands in the air!"

Dead silence.

Nigel stood at the prow, a rifle in hand. Bailey, Hayes, and Brillman were on his right; Stimson, Talmadge, Flummerfelt on his left. All armed.

"This is a mutiny!" Philip cried out, elbowing his way out from behind Nigel.

"I fink they caught that already," Nigel murmured.

Only Dr. Montfort dropped his pick. The rest of Barth's men were staring, stunned.

"Drop 'em, I told you!" Nigel shouted.

Kennedy was the first to laugh, a sudden explosive guffaw. Mansfield's shoulders began to quiver, and soon he, too, was laughing. Then Windham and Dr. Montfort.

Captain Barth strode toward the mutineers, his fists clenched. "What the hell is this, your idea of a joke?"

"*Stay back, I'm warning you!*" Philip shrieked. He held out a pistol that vibrated along with his hand.

Flummerfelt raised his rifle to the sky.

The sharp crack of the shot stopped Barth in his tracks. The laughter stopped, and all the men finally dropped their shovels and picks.

Colin swallowed hard.

"Captain . . ." Mansfield said cautiously.

Barth backed away. "You bastards."

"No, not us, Cap'n," Nigel said. "Ask your men who the villain is. Ask their opinion of you."

"Who's the leader of this circus — you?" Barth glanced from Nigel to Philip. "Or Little Lord Fauntleroy?"

"Not funny!" Philip blurted out.

"Shoot us," Mansfield said. "Go ahead. Then what'll you do? What'll you tell the others?"

"There are no others," Nigel replied. "The *Mystery* is going 'ome, gen'l'men, where she belongs."

"You won't get away with this," Barth said through clenched teeth.

"I don't believe you have the authority to determine that anymore." Philip stepped forward, gesturing toward the ladder with his pistol. "After you . . . Elias."

Captain Barth hauled back his fist but Dr.

Montfort caught him by the arm. "Do what he says, Captain," he said gently. "Please."

Yes, Colin thought. *Do it.*

Captain Barth walked stiffly up the ladder. Philip followed behind, grinning.

Nigel and his men forced the others up afterward. Colin was last. He felt the barrel of a gun against his back. "We can use the likes of you," Talmadge said. "Think about it."

Colin said nothing.

The men were facing amidships, their hands in the air. Philip pointed his gun at Barth's head.

"You imbecile!" Nigel called out. "Don't kill nobody yet!"

Philip ignored him. "Dress left!" he shouted to Barth. "And march!"

Captain Barth turned slowly and walked to the mainmast.

Philip kicked a wooden barrel toward him. "Climb it — keep your back against the mast."

Slowly Barth stood on the stool. Above his head, a halyard hung low, swinging in the wind.

Now Philip was climbing another barrel, next to Barth. With one hand on his pistol, he carefully attached the back of Barth's coat to the metal hook.

Then, stepping down, he kicked away both barrels.

Barth dropped.

His coat caught, and he hung from the hook, swinging above the deck.

"Happy New Year, deck rat," Philip said.

25

Andrew

December 31, 1909

He hadn't been able to sleep. It was too cold. He was worried. And now there was a smell. A hideous, powerful, human-waste kind of smell.

Andrew's eyes opened. The smell was coming from Lombardo. Lombardo had relieved himself but nobody had noticed it, they were all asleep like dead men.

He looked around, squinting at the still-lit sky through the cave.

A body was slumped in the opening.

"*Jack!*" Andrew leaped across the floor and pulled his stepfather back in, brushing off the snow, slapping his face. "Dr. Riesman! Somebody! *Help me!*"

Jack's skin was cold. He was breathing, but slowly.

Andrew threw the parka around him. He grabbed the nearest sleeping bag, Oppenheim's, and wrapped that around Jack, too. Oppenheim didn't flinch, didn't grumble.

They were immobile. All of them.

It was a mass polar sleep. A slaughter.

"Jack, wake up! *Somebody help me!*"

No answer.

Andrew set Jack down, tucking the sleeping bag around him, and ran outside to get the stove. He would heat up water — heat up something to keep Jack warm.

The dogs were gone.

The dogs were gone. How were the men going to get back now?

He ran for the supply tent. His foot jammed against something hard and he went sprawling.

Socrates lifted his head out of the snow. Nearby a tail popped out.

Of course. The dogs were buried. They were keeping warm.

"Good boy," Andrew said. "Stay. Just . . . stay."

He took the stove and ran back into the tent. Jack's head was moving now. He let out a moan, barely audible.

"Jack! Can you hear me?"

"Andrew?" Jack's eyes fluttered. "Andrew, go to sleep. Please. It's okay. I'll take the shift."

"Shift?"

"The night watch. I've got it under control. Just leave me. I'm fine. I'm feeling pretty good . . ." Jack's eyes began to close.

"There's not going to be a night watch. Get up, Jack. We're leaving."

"What?"

"Everybody up!" Andrew shouted. *"O'Malley, cook us something!"*

He was screaming now. He had no choice. This was not the place to sleep. It was not the time. They would die here, all of them. They needed to eat. The food stores were low, but rationing made no sense. They needed to eat it all, eke out what energy they could and move on — farther north, closer to the water, closer to the seals and penguins. Food.

"Will someone shut him up?" Cranston mumbled.

Ruppenthal yawned. "What stinks?"

"Come on, we're moving," Andrew said. He ran around the tent, shaking the men, glancing over his shoulder at Jack. "Move! Pop's orders — right, Pop?"

Jack wrapped himself tighter in his coverings. "Yes. Right."

Cranston was the first up, then Ruppenthal. Andrew kept shaking the others, one by one — all except Lombardo. He would have to be wrapped up and loaded onto a sledge, along with Kosta.

Soon the men were mobilizing. There was little protesting. Lombardo's stench was unbearable now. Thank goodness for Lombardo.

Just outside the cave, O'Malley set up his stove. The meat supply was low. He threw some pemmican to the dogs and cooked up the remaining steaks and chops for the men.

The sun was on its upward swing now, the clouds clearing. From the stove, smoke snaked into the cave, warming it quickly. Everyone was awake now, eating as much as his stomach could hold. Dr. Riesman fed himself and Lombardo.

Andrew kept Jack warm, bringing him food and hot coffee. They had plenty of coffee. It looked like bilge and tasted like gunpowder, but there was enough for the trip and more.

Jack's color returned slowly, but he was drowsy and weak. He would be in no condition to lead for a while.

"Siegal, Rivera," Andrew said. "Can you get a reading on our location? Petard, Ruskey, Cranston — harness the dogs and let's be ready to move."

"Yeah," Siegal muttered, shambling outside to find the sextant.

"Ruppenthal, Oppenheim, Dr. Riesman — let's strap Kosta and Lombardo on the sledges," Andrew said. "Jack?"

"I'll move on my own steam," Jack replied. He stood, propping himself up against the wall.

Soon Rivera called out, "We're due south of the ship, maybe eighty miles."

"A good week's travel and we'll be back," Siegal added. "If the weather holds."

"That's a laugh," Oppenheim said.

They wouldn't have a week. Andrew knew that in his bones. One more week of this, and they'd all be dead.

They'd have to cover twenty miles a day, at least. And find some food on the way.

They prepared quickly, packing the sleeping bags, the stove, and the meager store of food.

Kosta protested that he could walk, but on his first attempt he fell into the snow with a howl, upsetting the dogs.

He would remain sledgebound, like it or not.

Lombardo had lapsed back into unconsciousness.

The men strapped the two invalids onto sledges. Jack took the reins of Lombardo's sledge, Andrew the other.

The dogs seemed refreshed by the sleep and the meal, but they still moved slowly.

Jack was falling asleep at the reins of the other sledge. The men were sliding along listlessly, stooped over their skis.

To the north-northwest a low, dense white cloud was sweeping toward them across the plain.

"Heeyah!" Andrew shouted, pulling on the reins.

Eighty miles.

26

Colin

December 31, 1909

"What in the blazes do you think you're doing?"

Mansfield was spitting mad. Ignoring the circle of rifles, he grabbed a barrel, climbed up, and unhooked Captain Barth.

The Captain fell to the deck.

Nigel reared back and swung the butt of his rifle at Mansfield. It hit the back of his head with a loud crack, and he crumpled beside Barth.

"*That's* wha' we're doin'," Nigel said. "An' we'll do it to anyone wha' stands in our way. Don't matter who it is. New rules of the sea, gen'l'men.

Survival of the fittest. These is neutrical waters, an' Captain Barf has no jurisdinction."

Barth was cradling Mansfield's head in his lap. "What do you suppose will happen when we arrive home, Nigel?" he said bitterly. "They'll let you go scot-free?"

"I won't be on board, *Elias*," Nigel replied. "Because the ship will be makin' a few stops first. Australia, I figure, would be just the right place for my good friend Philip and me to set up a new life. My mates 'ere will keep the officials busy wif stories of their 'eroism while we slip away. Eventually someone will find you — if you're still alive. Then you can give your side of the story and see who listens, let the world judge your American imperialist propagan —"

"Nigel, will you shut up and throw them in the brig!" Philip blurted out.

"Right," Nigel snapped. "Line 'em up, Brillman."

"Aren't we going to give 'em a chance to join us?" Brillman asked.

"Let *me* do the finkin', will you?" Nigel said.

Brillman gestured meekly with his rifle. "Sorry about this, guys. Go on, now. Get down there."

"Not like that," Nigel said with disgust. "Like this."

He gave Kennedy a swift kick in the pants. Kennedy flew across the deck, nearly falling down the hatch stairs.

Windham lunged for Nigel. "You sniveling little —"

Flummerfelt grabbed Windham by the scruff of the neck and threw him across the deck.

Colin shot him a glance. He hadn't expected this. Not at all.

Flummerfelt looked away uneasily.

"Right," Nigel said. "Now get into the brig, all of you!"

Colin fell into line. He followed the other men down the ladder, across the afterhold, and then down into the storage hold.

Abaft, in a dark corner of the ship, were three closetlike rooms with barred doors.

"You first, Elias." Philip prodded Captain Barth in the back with his pistol.

Colin eyed Flummerfelt. He was scowling, his eyes darting around the room.

His gun was loaded, but he wouldn't shoot down here. Not belowdecks, in close quarters. Especially not in a place where a bullet could cause a leak.

Captain Barth was stepping toward the brig, his face sagging with the humiliation.

It was time.

Colin stepped in front of Barth. Calmly he faced down the barrel of Philip's pistol. "I'm afraid you'll have to shoot me first, Philip."

"Winslow, don't be a fool!" Barth tried to push him aside, but Colin held his ground.

The men were all shouting, warning Colin to move aside. For his own good.

Philip pointed the pistol at Colin's head. "Feeling brave? Do you think I wouldn't shoot you?"

"Is that what you said to the bank officers?" Colin replied.

"The *who*?"

"At the Bank of London?"

Philip blanched. "What are you talking about?"

"It's in all the newspapers — right, Nigel? The ones that call Philip an upper-class thief, considered armed and dangerous because he stole ten thousand pounds from the bank? You know, the papers you found in Philip's footlocker?"

Philip shot a glance at Nigel. "You — you looked in my *footlocker*? You showed them to *him*? Those are my intimate possessions!"

"Rot!" Nigel yelled. "I did no such a fing!"

Slowly Flummerfelt backed into the shadows.

"What did Nigel promise you, Philip?" Colin said. "He'd keep your dirty secret if you went along with him? How much is he in for, thirty percent? Fifty? And you really think he'll follow through? You think he won't turn you in the minute you set foot on shore?"

Philip cocked the trigger. His face was red. "*Get . . . in . . . the . . . brig.*"

"The secret's out, Philip," Colin said. "We all know now. You're in trouble no matter what. Go ahead and shoot me, if you want. Shoot us all — then you and your friends can take the ship home by yourselves, just the way you planned. Or are you too cowardly for that?"

"You want to see how cowardly I am? *Do* you?"

"DON'T!" Mansfield yelled, diving across the floor.

Philip pulled the trigger.

The gun exploded.

Colin collapsed. He clasped his hand to his head and felt blood.

Mansfield landed hard on Philip — and the room broke into chaos.

In the dim light Colin turned. His eyes saw double. He could make out Mansfield pounding

Philip. The other men were jumping on one another, banging against the walls of the close space.

Colin felt the side of his forehead. It had hurt. Much more than he'd expected.

Gunpowder. The rifle had had gunpowder and . . .

What?

Flummerfelt was charging around the corner now, carrying six rifles, each with a red ribbon around its barrel. Colin struggled to his feet and elbowed his way through the crowd.

"You nearly had me killed," Colin said.

Flummerfelt shoved three rifles toward him. "These are loaded! I tied the ribbons around so we'd know!"

"You were supposed to *empty* the others!"

"I put grain in some of them, packed it in good. Left in a tiny bit of gunpowder — you know, for the effect."

"Any more, and my head would have been blood pudding. Now, come on!"

The men were brawling on a deck slippery with wheat and barley. Colin handed a rifle to Captain Barth and another to Windham.

"Flummerfelt's one of us!" Colin shouted. "These are —"

The crack of a rifle cut him off.

"— loaded," Colin continued.

The deck went silent.

Flummerfelt was looking sheepishly at a hole in the ship's hull. His rifle was smoking. "Um, I think it's above the waterline. Sorry."

Colin gestured toward Philip with his rifle. "Into the brig. You first."

Philip spun around on Nigel. "You had to open your big mouth."

"Me?" Nigel replied. "Wha' 'appened to the guns? You was supposed to make sure the guns was ready."

"How could I? *You* were talking so much, lecturing me with your dreary social philosophy, regaling everyone else with tales of my youthful exploits in London. No wonder they were able to sabotage us right under my nose —"

"*Your* nose is always so bloody 'igh in the air —"

"Will you shut your traps?" Kennedy said.

The carpenter hauled off and gave Nigel a good kick in the pants, to a rousing cheer from the men.

"I'll bring you up on charges!" Nigel screamed.

Colin and Captain Barth pushed him into one of the cages. The other men followed meekly.

With a flourish, Captain Barth slammed the doors and closed the locks.

The mutiny was over.

"'Attaboy, mate," Windham said.

"Three cheers for Colin Winslow!" Kennedy bellowed.

"Our new third-in-command, after Mansfield," Captain Barth said, "if he'll agree."

"Hip hip —"

"HOORAY!"

"Hip hip —"

"HOORAY!"

"Hip hip —"

"HOORAY!"

"Third in command?" Colin said. "I couldn't . . ."

Barth put his hand on Colin's shoulder and smiled. "You have a while to think it over. No matter what you decide, you can be sure your father will hear about this. Now, let's get this ship moving so we can celebrate the beginning of 1910!"

Colin wanted to feel triumphant but couldn't. There were now six men to run the ship. Six men to keep her out of the ice while they waited for Father.

Assuming Father returned.

27

Andrew

January 2, 1910

"Go! You find Papa! Later!"

Later? It was easy for Kosta to say. He was lying on the sledge. He was cargo. He didn't have to be up here facing the blizzard.

Andrew squinted into the blinding snow. The other sledge was gone. It had been next to him a moment earlier, and now it was gone.

Jack had told him they were getting closer to the sea, maybe one day away, maybe three, he wasn't sure because he couldn't take any readings, because the compass was lost, and so were the sun and the horizon.

And now that they'd come this far, now that

they had a chance of making it back alive, they had loosened up too much, let themselves stray away from each other.

The two sledges were not supposed to separate. One had the food and tents, the other had most of the equipment. Now Andrew couldn't eat or pitch a camp. Jack couldn't cook.

Brilliant. Just brilliant.

Whose idea was this? What kind of stupid planning was this?

Jack might be ten yards away — or a mile. In this weather, you couldn't tell. Andrew pulled the dogs in a wide circle. They were shuffling. They had no energy. If only Socrates were among them. If only Jack hadn't taken him. "Come on, Dimitriou! Foti! Yiorgo! Move it! Go!"

The terrain was rough, piled with icy snow, old pressure ridges. The dogs were slipping, tangling up in their traces, slowing everything down.

Slowing down meant losing time. Losing time meant failure.

"*Pethaino!*" Kosta yelled.

"Shut up, you're not dying!" Andrew said. "We're going to make it!"

He was sick of Kosta. For hours Kosta had lain on the sledge, shivering and groaning, demanding and complaining — as if there were something more Andrew could do. As if Andrew hadn't already taken the tarpaulin from the sledge and wrapped Kosta in it. As if the snow wasn't hitting him like shrapnel and the wind shearing the skin from his face and the dogs putting out about as much energy as field mice.

"What else do you want me to do?" Andrew shouted.

"*Ti?*" Kosta asked.

Nothing.

Never mind.

This was hopeless.

The whole damn thing was hopeless.

The sledge was expendable now. The dogs were a burden.

Kosta was a burden.

There would be no overnight shelter now. The entire distance would have to be covered without sleep. In one long trek.

But not at this pace. At this pace they wouldn't make it.

He could move faster by himself. He'd have to, if he wanted to live. He could reach the *Mystery* and send back a search party.

He halted the sledge and climbed off.

His skis stuck out the back of the equipment pile, caked with snow. Andrew brushed them off and began putting them on his feet.

"You go?" Kosta asked.

"Yes," Andrew said.

"*Kalòs*. Good."

Good. Such selflessness. Such a martyr.

The poles were in fine shape. Barring any invisible crevasses, he could make a minimum of fifteen miles a day, maybe double that if it were sunny.

"Andreou?"

"What?"

"Put near dogs. Me die with dogs."

"Kosta, stop saying that. You are not going to —"

"*Se parakalo!* Please!"

This was it. The last demand.

Andrew hooked his arms under Kosta and lifted.

He could feel the older man shivering, praying under his breath: *Pater imon, o entis ouranis . . .*

Andrew didn't know the words, but there was no mistaking the rhythm. *Our Father, who art in heaven . . .*

The prayer seemed quaint and distant. He hadn't prayed since Mother's death, hadn't thought of it. But as Kosta chanted, the words came to Andrew from far away, from a church and a Sunday school that seemed to be in another life. A life he'd never have again. Never. Even if he did survive.

They were just words now. Words and time. Kosta was heavy, so heavy, and Andrew knew this delay could cost him, this could be the difference between survival and *Thy kingdom come . . .*

Thy will be done, on earth as it is in heaven. . . .

But what about here? What about Antarctica? Where was God's will now? Was He watching over the cold and the snow and the slow, agonizing deaths and saying, *Lo, it is good?* Was this how He rewarded faith?

Faith was the key to the kingdom, Mother always said. Faith, hope, love. Without them, we might as well be stones in the river. Beasts of the field.

Well, faith hadn't stopped the snow. Hope hadn't kept the sledges together or saved Shreve. The God of mercy did nothing but watch while men's blood slowly turned to ice. Faith and hope were suckers' games.

Deliver us from evil, for Thine is the kingdom and the power and the glory forever . . .

And suddenly Andrew felt the ice on his face,

the rivulet freezing down his cheek, and he was crying, holding Kosta in his arms and crying, and he didn't know how he'd gotten there, how he'd ended up at the bottom of the world dragging a man through the snow so he could die with his dogs.

A man who had once saved his life.

"Peegheneh, paithì mou."

"I — I —" Andrew said.

"You go, Andreou!"

"I can't."

Kosta had sacrificed. The dogs had sacrificed. Andrew couldn't turn his back on them.

He turned, pulling Kosta around.

Kosta protested. He told Andrew to leave him. He used many Greek words that Andrew had never heard — blunt words, definitely not biblical.

But he stopped fighting as Andrew loaded him onto the sledge.

"We go," Andrew said. "Together. *Mazì*. Okay?"

"*Mazì*," Kosta replied.

They would have to travel lighter. Andrew ran around to the back of the sledge and began unloading things they didn't need: snowshoes . . . skis . . . packs . . . books . . . microscope . . . medical supplies.

He kept the sextant. The Primus stove. One club and one rifle. Enough equipment for two.

The compass was gone. They'd have to go by wind direction. Jack had said the wind was coming from the north. But that was a while ago. Without landmarks, it was impossible to tell if the direction had changed.

Andrew would have to head into the wind and hope. At least until the sun was visible.

"Let's go!"

The dogs dug in. Andrew leaped onto the sledge, yanked the reins, and braced himself.

The wind was brutal. It shoved the breath back down his throat. He had to drop his head, keeping the top of his hood to the wind.

Andrew felt his eyelids droop and he jerked his head back. He would not fall into the trap. He knew better now.

He jumped off the sledge and started to walk. Without his weight, the dogs immediately picked up speed.

Good. They would force him to keep up. You couldn't fall asleep while you were walking.

He grabbed hold of the supply pile, put his head to the wind, and trudged forward.

The snow sprayed out from beneath the sledge

runners, hissing rhythmically, and he thought of his Flexible Flyer racing through the Boston Commons, how scary that seemed back then, how simple life used to be, back before the fights and the police station, before Jack and Colin and all the good years in New York, before the plans for the trip and Mother's pneumonia.

It was all connected somehow, all the happiness and grief, so that this moment and all those moments occupied the same space, and his life was not a long string of events but one point in time, all ages existing at once.

Another day or two, that was all. He'd be on the *Mystery* again, heading back to that life. Back to home and warmth, food and poetry, paved streets and parks, hearthstones and hobs, hospitals and horses and gas lamps and automobiles and evening clothes and soot and outings and music and wouldn't Brahms be good now — death and life touched each other in his music, in his soul — the voices lifting up, singing: *Tod, wo ist dein Stachel!* Death, where is thy sting?

Where indeed.

For a while Andrew's feet moved. Then they didn't.

28

Colin

January 8, 1910

His heart was beating.

He looked dead and his skin was bone-white, but Colin saw that his heart was beating.

Colin glanced over his shoulder, but no one was there. They had taken the Greek back with the sledge.

They hadn't even seen Andrew in the snow.

He lowered his shoulder, lifted his stepbrother's arm, and hoisted him up with such force that Andrew almost flew over.

He was the weight of a lashed foresail. He needed food badly. Food and warmth.

Leaning slightly forward, Colin held Andrew

across his shoulders, linking his arms behind Andrew's knees and neck. Carefully he retraced his footsteps. They led to a mound of ice, about chest high, connected by wire to another mound about fifteen yards away. It was the end of a row of cairns that extended outward from the *Mystery* for maybe 200 yards. The cairns had been Colin's idea. Several rows of them radiated out from the ship, like spokes from an axle. They served as guides for anyone caught in a blinding storm.

Had Andrew stayed on his feet for another few moments, he would have spotted this one.

The *Mystery* soon came into sight. The men were passing Kosta up and over the gunwale. The dogs waited on their haunches, emaciated and dazed.

Mansfield and Flummerfelt offered to help with Andrew, but Colin walked him up alone.

Captain Barth was waiting at the top. "How is he?"

"Alive," Colin replied.

"We have a makeshift hospital in the afterhold. Dr. Montfort will look at him right away. We've set up a cot next to your father."

"My father? He's —?"

Barth nodded. "Alive. Awake. Flummerfelt found the other sledge. Off starboard bow. With all the men. They were wandering, looking for Andrew. Somehow he'd separated from the others. Your father wanted to stay out and find him. Flummerfelt practically had to wrestle him back here."

Colin carefully descended the stairs. The afterhold deck had been cleared, and the expeditioners were laid out head to toe. Three cots were off to the port side. Father and Kosta rested on two of them. Colin lay Andrew on the other.

Dr. Montfort, who had been dressing the wounds on Kosta's feet, immediately shifted to Andrew, checking his pulse and lifting his eyelids. "Windham, get this boy some food and liquid!"

Windham rushed in with a kettle of tea and a plate of exquisite-smelling fried food.

"What's that?" Colin asked.

"Crispy penguin fritters," Windham said. "You haven't lived until you've tried them."

"For the moment," Dr. Montfort said, "we'll see how he takes the fluids."

Colin knelt by Father, cringing at the sight of his face. His cheeks were covered with dry, black, angry-looking blotches. His eyelids were swollen and his lips badly chapped. His eyes fluttered open.

"Colin?"

"Yes, Father."

"Where's Andrew?"

"Next to you, Father. He's going to be okay, I think."

"Thank God," Father said, his voice heavy and slow. "I — I was with him. He was right beside me . . . I let him out of my sight. . . ."

Colin took his hand. "Don't worry. Everybody survived."

"No. Not everybody."

Colin carefully counted heads. "Thirteen," he said. "Who's missing?"

"Shreve," Father said. "We lost him. I let him go, too. This is all . . . my fault. . . ."

"Father, stop it. Go to sleep, okay?"

". . . You were right. . . ." Father's voice was drifting in and out, woozy and dreamlike. "You . . . you didn't want to do this, Colin. You didn't want to go . . . and you were so right. . . ."

Colin had to turn away. Father was crying.

Shock. Frostbite. Exposure. He wasn't himself. He needed sleep. The experience had affected his mind.

Colin felt his own eyes water. All of the men looked like Father, or worse. Like they'd been swallowed up by death and spit back out.

Above them, the dogs' paws clickety-clacked

against the decking as they settled into their kennels. They looked awful, too. Colin hadn't recognized any of them. One was descending the stairs now, wagging its tail, holding a rag in its mouth.

No. Not a rag. A doll. A Greek soldier.

The dog bounded across the floor and started slobbering all over Andrew.

"Hey — get away!" Colin shouted.

Andrew's eyes opened. He smiled and whispered, "Socrates," and he threw his arms around the dog's neck as it licked every inch of his scabby face.

Colin grinned. "Hey, no need to thank me, Andrew. Saving your life is my life's business."

Andrew threw off Socrates and propped himself up on his elbows. "Colin?"

"Happy New Year," Colin said. "You made it. So did Father. But don't wake him up just yet. He's a little off his beam."

Andrew turned and let out a sudden sob. He reached out to touch Jack's face. "His face —"

"Frostbite," Colin said. "You have it, too."

"I do?"

"Don't touch. Not to worry, you're back on the *Mystery* now, under improved management." Colin reached for Windham's platter. "Care for some tea and penguin fritters?"

29

Andrew

January 8, 1910

It hurt.

It hurt so much to smile.

"He slapped my face," Jack was saying. "I had crossed over to Neverland, and Andrew pummeled me back to life. I nearly slugged him."

"We all felt like doing that," Rivera said.

Ruppenthal nodded. "He's a lousy sailor, he can't tell a joke, and he got lost twice — but yeah, okay, we all would have died without him."

"Hear, hear!" Ruskey called out.

"I didn't mean to wake *you* up in the cave, Ruppenthal," Andrew said.

The men roared. Andrew was shocked. He'd never made them laugh before.

Even Colin was chuckling. A little.

The expedition team members were all awake now. Oppenheim and Cranston were silent and listless, Lombardo was fading in and out, and Kosta was trying hard not to show that he was in pain. But the rest had regained a bit of their old selves.

Jack had told Captain Barth and the crew all about the trip — exaggerating Andrew's role shamelessly, of course. But that was all right.

The smell of cooked seal was heavy in the room now. Windham stepped out of the galley with a platter full of steaks, yellow and blubbery-looking. "Come 'n' get 'em while they're hot!"

Andrew had never enjoyed anything so revolting-looking before. The expeditioners were slavering at their plates, bolting the stuff down as if it were filet mignon.

The *Mystery* crew — seven of the ones who'd remained behind — all stared at them agape.

"Well, gentlemen," Captain Barth announced. "Speaking of tales of derring-do, perhaps you may be wondering why the crew seems a bit . . . shorthanded."

Barth followed with a story so absurd that if it

hadn't come from his mouth, Andrew would not have believed it. When Barth got to the part about the wheat and barley, Andrew almost burst out laughing — but Barth's expression stopped him.

"I never thought I could be fooled by the likes of a Nigel or Philip," Barth said. "Colin Winslow, gentlemen, is the reason this ship was here when you arrived. He saved your lives."

"Colin, this is extraordinary," Jack said.

Colin shrugged. "Flummerfelt did most of the work —"

"I was on their side before you stepped in," Flummerfelt reminded him.

"Nigel didn't plan well," Colin said. "And Philip — well, he's Philip, and —"

"For God's sake, take the credit!" Lombardo said, and he began to sing faintly: "Forrr . . . he's a jolly good fe-e-ellow, for he's a jolly good fe-e-ellow . . ."

Jack reached out and put an arm around Colin. "You deserve it, son."

Colin flinched.

His father pulled him into an embrace. Colin looked awkward and uncomfortable.

But he didn't pull back. And he didn't look angry. He actually seemed to be enjoying it. A little.

Andrew smiled. This was promising.

"Well, eat up, everyone!" Captain Barth said. "I'm going to check on our prisoners, let them know what's happened — and tomorrow we attempt again to break through the —"

CRRRRRRRRACKKKK!

The cots began to tilt. The dogs leaped to their feet and howled.

The ship was moving. Lifting to port.

Captain Barth ran upstairs to the deck. Mansfield followed hard on his heels.

Jack's face lost whatever color it had regained. "What's the report, Elias?" he called out.

"I was afraid of this!" Barth shouted. "The wind has shifted — it's blowing the pack ice in from the northeast!"

"Is there damage?" Colin asked.

Mansfield clattered down the stairs. "Not yet. But we've got pressure on the bow and stern — two floes moving against the ship, pushing her upward on the port side."

"Another on starboard!" Captain Barth added.

"Can we move her?" Jack said.

"If the wind changes, the pressure'll let up. Or at least we can try to chop her out."

"And if the wind keeps up?" Andrew asked.

"She's a strong ship," Mansfield replied. "Ain't none built thicker. But she's trapped between the floes. We've got to act as soon as we can, or else the ice will . . ."

He fell silent.

No one had the guts to ask him to finish. Either that, or they already knew the answer.

"The ice will what?" Colin asked.

Mansfield swallowed hard. "It'll cut her in half."

TO BE CONTINUED IN

Escape from Disaster

Glossary

abaft — toward the aft

aft — the rear of a ship, or stern

amidships — in the center of a ship

barque — a three- to five-masted ship with all masts square-rigged except the aftermast, which is fore-and-aft rigged

barquentine — a three- to five-masted ship with a square-rigged foremast but fore-and-aft rigged mainmast and mizzenmast

batten (n) — a narrow wooden strip of wood

batten (v) — to fasten or secure with a batten

bilge — the lowest part of a ship's hull

bilge pump — a pump to rid the bilge of water that has leaked in

boom — the horizontal spar used to support the bottom edge of a sail

bow — the front of a ship

bowsprit — the spar extending from the bow of a ship

brash ice — ground-up ice floes and lumps of snow with a puddinglike texture

bulkhead — an upright partition that separates compartments of a ship

bulwarks — the sides of a ship, above the upper deck
cairn — a pile of stones used as a landmark
calve (v) — to break off (as in a mass of ice)
come about — to change direction by tacking
crosstrees — the intersection of the mast and the yardarm, on a full-rigged mast
crosswind — a wind that blows *across* a ship, as opposed to a *tailwind* or *headwind*
encroach — to move in beyond the usual boundaries
fo'c'sle — short for *forecastle*; the crew's quarters, usually in a ship's bow
foremast — the mast at the bow end of a ship
foretop — the platform at the top of the foremast on a square-rigged ship
freshening wind — a wind whose strength is increasing
fulmar — a seabird related to the *petrel*
gaff-rigged — an arrangement of sails in which a slanted spar (an extension from the mast) supports the top side of the sail
galley — a ship's kitchen
gallows — the enclosed storage area for spare masts and sails
greenheart — a dark greenish wood, known for its durability, from a South American evergreen tree
groaner — an ice floe that makes a groaning sound as it grinds against the edge of another floe

gunwale — the highest edge of a ship's hull
halyard — the rope used to raise sails
hardtack — a hard, plain biscuit made of flour and water
heave to (past tense, *hove to*) — to turn a ship's bow into the wind and let the ship stay adrift in preparation for a storm
heel (v) — to lean to one side due to wind or waves
high following sea — how the sea appears behind a ship when it is traveling down a swell
hob — a protrusion over or in a fireplace on which to hang an object to be heated
hull — the frame, or body, of a ship
hummock — a ridge of ice
iceberg — a large mass of floating ice broken off (*calved*) from shelf ice or from a glacier
ice floe — a flat, floating fragment of sea ice
ice flower — a flowerlike formation of ice, sometimes occurring in fields
ice shelf (also *shelf ice*) — an ice sheet that begins on land and extends into the water, resting on the sea bottom
ice shower — frozen mist falling to the earth as ice crystals
jib — a triangular sail at the bow, supported at the bottom by a jibboom

jibe — to move sails from one side to the other while sailing into the wind in order to change a ship's direction

keel — the central timber at the bottom of a ship, running from bow to stern

lay to — to bring a ship to a stop in open water, facing the wind

lead (n) — a path of water through pack ice

leaden sea — dull gray sea

lee — the side sheltered from the wind

list (v) — to tilt to one side

mainmast — the second mast from the bow after foremast (middle mast on the *Mystery*)

mainsail — the bottom sail on the mainmast

mast — the vertical pole that supports sails

mizzenmast (or *mizzen*) — the sail on the aft end of a ship (the third sail on the *Mystery*)

mush — to travel over snow with a dogsled

nor'easter — a strong wind from the northeast, usually accompanied by a storm

old ice — ice floes that have remained unmelted from previous seasons, usually dense and hummocky

pack ice — a mass of floating ice caused by the crushing together of floes and brash

pancake ice — seawater frozen into patches of rubbery consistency

pea coat — a short, double-breasted, heavy woolen coat worn by sailors

pemmican — food made from dried beef and filler such as flour, molasses, or dried fruit

petrel — a small, long-winged bird

port — the left side of a ship (as you face the bow)

pressure ridge — ice that has been pushed upward between colliding ice floes

Primus stove — a small, portable metal stove consisting of one burner and a wire platform over it

pudding ice — see *brash ice*

rigging — the arrangement of sails, spars, and ropes

rime — tufts of ice or frost formed by water vapor freezing on contact with a solid object

rudder — a plate mounted at the ship's stern for directing its course

sastruga (pl., *sastrugi*) — a long wavelike ridge of snow, formed by the wind

sheet — a rope, attached to the bottom of a sail, used to change the angle of the angle relative to the wind

ship water (v) — to take in water over the ship's hull

short-sail — less then a full arrangement of sails

sledge — a sled used for transporting loads over the ice

spar — a pole that supports sails and rigging

square-rigged — an arrangement of square-shaped sails

starboard — the right side of a ship (as you face the bow)

stave in (past tense, *stove in*) — to smash or crush inward

staysail — a triangular sail supported by a rope (a stay) instead of a mast

stream ice — pack ice containing leads

tack — to change the direction of a ship, usually by turning the bow into the wind

taffrail — the rail at the stern of a ship

tiller — a lever with which to turn a rudder and steer a boat

trace(s) — strap(s) connecting a harnessed dog to a sledge

water sky — a dark streak on the horizon that indicates open ocean

wheelhouse — an enclosed area from which a ship is controlled when under way

windward — the side exposed to the wind (opposite of *leeward*)

yardarm — the spar that supports the top edge of a square sail

young ice — brittle, newly formed sea ice, one or two feet thick

Bibliography

Alexander, Caroline. *Endurance: Shackleton's Legendary Antarctic Expedition.* Alfred A. Knopf, 1999. Excellent reproductions of Antarctic photos taken by master polar photographer Frank Hurley.

Armstrong, Jennifer. *Shipwreck at the Bottom of the World: Shackleton's Amazing Voyage.* Crown Publishers, 1998.

Bickel, Leonard. *Mawson's Will.* Avon Books, 1977. Thrilling survival story; Douglas Mawson walked 320 miles across Antarctica after a companion and all his dogs and equipment fell into a crevasse.

Cherry-Garrard, Apsley. *The Worst Journey in the World.* Carroll & Graf, 1989. Robert Falcon Scott's fatal voyage to the South Pole.

Huntford, Roland. *Scott & Amundsen.* G. P. Putnam's Sons, 1980. The race between Scott and Amundsen for the South Pole, with photos and maps.

Lansing, Alfred. *Endurance: Shackleton's Incredible Voyage.* Carroll & Graf, 1986. Thrilling, vivid, true story of the sinking of Shackleton's ship and the uncanny survival and rescue of all his men.

Maloney, Elbert S. *Chapman Piloting.* Hearst Marine

Books (various ed.). Good book for basic sailing information.
Shackleton, Ernest. *South*. Carroll & Graf, 1998. A memoir of the voyage of the *Endurance* by its legendary leader. Full of interesting details.
Worsley, F. A. *Shackleton's Boat Journey*. W. W. Norton & Company, 1977. Written by the captain of the *Endurance*, an account of what many call the greatest boat journey in the world, by Shackleton, Worsley, and four other men, across the Drake Passage on a modified 22-foot lifeboat.

Websites:

www.ista.co.uk.com. Diagrams and terminology for various sailing ships and rigs.
www.pbs.org/wgbh/nova/shackleton. An excellent web documentary of Shackleton's fabled transantarctic voyage, contemporary adventures, and lots of good general information about Antarctica. Video clips.
www.terraquest.com/antarctica/index.html. An excellent and exciting introduction to Antarctica with good images.
www.theice.org. Facts and figures about Antarctica.

About the Author

Peter Lerangis is the author of the award-winning sci-fi/mystery series *Watchers*, the first book of which earned a 1999 Quick Pick for Young Adult Reluctant Readers award. His classic YA thrillers, *The Yearbook* and *Driver's Dead*, have been enjoyed in this country and throughout the world. His recent movie adaptations include *The Sixth Sense*, *El Dorado*, and *Sleepy Hollow*. Peter is a Harvard graduate with a degree in biochemistry and experience as a Broadway actor, which he feels are eminent qualifications for writing fiction. He lives in New York City with his wife, Tina deVaron, and their two sons, Nick and Joe.